# ZOMBIE SCOUT

## THE DIARY OF JACK SULLIVAN

A Novel by R. Diskin Black

ISBN: 0-615-75263-2
ISBN-13: 978-0-615-75263-1

*- for my brother -*

# HOBOKEN, NEW JERSEY
## *4 months, 2 weeks & 5 days after the first reported incident*

*Tuesday, May 23, 2017*

Not the way I expected to spend my fourteenth birthday, hanging out in a tower with a pair of binoculars looking for zombies. But then nothing is the way it was back in January when this nightmare began. I tried to start a journal a couple of times the past few months - be all Anne Frank about my predicament - except whenever I looked down at the blank page nothing came out. So each time I put the notebook away and got on with the business of surviving. Until today, when I had to write. Because today I killed my first one. Well, not exactly "killed", since she was already dead. Still, I feel bad that it was a girl. Used to be a girl, I mean.

When she ran howling and clawing toward Jason, that way they do, I had all of one second to make up my mind to swing the ax I was carrying and smash her skull open. It was weird how once I started swinging I couldn't stop, probably a dozen extra swings after I had already pounded her head into oblivion. It definitely felt good at the time, even if I felt like crap later. As if I had really killed someone. But she had stopped being a "someone" long before Jason and I ran into her. It's the last time I let that jerk talk me into sneaking out of the city through the sewers for supplies without at least two others as backup. Man, she moved fast. Anyone who's ever seen an old black and white zombie movie where they lumber after you with arms outstretched moaning for brains would be shit out of luck encountering one of these ghouls.

I guess I should add if you're reading this in the future - listen, I really never cursed so much before the zom (our shorthand nickname for them). Really. Nice Catholic schoolboy, that was me. Now I'm a zombie scout. One of the best. Certainly better than Jason. Oh, before I forget, my name is Sullivan. Jack Sullivan. Did that sound too Bond, James Bond of me? I'm beginning this diary - yeah, I think I prefer diary to journal - at 6:46 p.m. on Tuesday, May 23, 2017 in Hoboken, New Jersey. OK, my writing break is over. I promise to write more later. I promise I won't die. I promise I won't become one of them. I hear them now howling from over the hill in Jersey City. You never get used to the howling, the "guttural moaning" I heard someone call it today. You never get used to the sound of them coming.

*Wednesday, May 24, 2017*

If I'm going to write this I may as well do it correctly, give the entire history as to how we find ourselves here now. When the television news began reporting on the "riots" in Central Asia right after the New Year, no one thought too much about it. After all, the world is a powder keg, especially that part of it. But a week or so before the television cut off in late February, I watched a show on CNN with a bunch of experts analyzing the events of those last few months, trying to figure out exactly what had happened. I remember that night so clearly. My younger brother, Ben, and I had just come back from seeing the 20th Anniversary re-release of *Titanic* with my Uncle Matt. The original is much better than that lame 3D version a few years ago, which I will confess I never even bothered to see. Watching those poor people drown in 3D is not really my thing. It was pretty cool, though, to see *Titanic* on a big screen the way it was originally shown, knowing it was the first movie Mom and Dad went to see together in a theater when they met. Anyway, I'm off the subject. I do that a lot.

All these experts on CNN agreed that the first zombie outbreak occurred on Thursday, January 5, 2017, on The Friendship Bridge that connects Uzbekistan and Afghanistan. Kind of ironic that the first time dead people started to bite living people in real life happened on a bridge called Friendship. Crazy, man. Who knows how and why it happened there at that precise moment in time? Sure, it's caused by a virus. At least, we think it is. Actually, we have no idea. But that's what they were saying on the evening news when we still had evening news. Other than that, no answers have come so far as to the how and why. After The Friendship Bridge Massacre, the Uzbeki Uprising began in Termez. Only it wasn't an uprising at all. The newspapers and cable stations got that all wrong because Uzbekistan had been pretty much shut off from the outside world for over three years, despite the presence of The Friendship Bridge.

On January 13th - Friday, the 13th for those of you who are superstitious - after a solid week of reports of riots across Kazakhstan, Turkmenistan and the Democratic Republic of Iran, the entire world was watching as a wild looking guy covered in blood burst into the opening of Parliament for the newly independent Democratic Republic of Chechnya. With all the bloodshed it took over the years to form that country, people figured at first it was just one more terrorist. But the cameras kept rolling as he bit two people and they bit two people and so on and so on and so on. . . .

We lived in our American bubble - that's what Dad always called it - for just a little while longer as the zombie outbreak spread across Europe and Asia like wildfire. Moscow, St. Petersburg, Kiev, Bucharest, Warsaw, Vienna, Berlin, and Paris spreading north and west. Kabul, Islamabad, New Delhi, Calcutta, Dhaka, Beijing, Pyongyang, and Seoul heading south and east. I felt really bad about Korea, that big ceremony on New Year's Day for reunification and the country doesn't even make it to the end of the month. I know. Crazy, man.

Then in mid February a passenger getting off a plane from Rio de Janero at Kennedy Airport - "Passenger Zero" - went berserk and it was over. It had reached South America and it reached New York, despite all those "expert" precautions they lectured us about for a month. Yeah, right. Like this could have been prevented. Since the entire world gathered in Rio last summer for the Olympics, I think that's when it happened there. Or at least that's when the seeds were sown. The "virus" must have, at first, had the ability to lay dormant for several months. Though I could be wrong. Maybe it wasn't the Olympics. It really doesn't matter. Does it? I have to run now. Scout duty. Will finish this sad tale tomorrow.

## Thursday, May 25, 2017

Dad should have made up his mind to stop going to work in the city the moment that guy landed at Kennedy. No matter what. But they said on the news that it was an isolated incident, which had been contained. And for twenty-four hours there were no more reports in the New York metropolitan area. A lot of people were working from home at that point, telecommuting with their iCards. Dad promised

Mom he would be home by lunchtime. Just one last trip across the Hudson to his office to gather some important files that still had not been iChived. He was going to meet Uncle Matt at Battery Park City and they were going to come home to us on a ferry with Tolstoy (Uncle Matt's cat).

That morning was the last time Ben, Mom or I saw Dad. He never returned with Uncle Matt and Tolstoy. He left us alone. Left me to be the man of the house. Lawyers are so stupid. They think nothing will ever happen to them. I'm sorry Dad, but you shouldn't have gone into the city that day. You should have stayed in Hoboken and had Uncle Matt come to us as soon as he woke up in the morning. I don't like being angry at you, Dad, but I am. Maybe you're still alive somewhere in New York. Mom holds on to that. I think sometimes it's all that gets her through the day. I don't know whether I believe you're alive or not. I suppose what I believe doesn't really matter. Whatever it is, it is. Wouldn't have talked like that five months ago.

Friday, May 26, 2017

Four straight days of writing. Cool, huh? I'm really impressing myself. Let's see if this continues. I promised Mom today that I would never leave Hoboken again through the sewers. She found out from Jason's mother what happened, though the part about me "killing" the girl seems not to bother her so much. She seems to only be concerned with my safety and welfare. I didn't even try to talk to her about it. I just nodded in agreement when she said "never again" before returning to her room and shutting the door.

It's late now, about fifteen minutes to midnight. I'm looking out my bedroom window across the Hudson to Manhattan. The fires are still burning. New York has been reduced to a smoldering, howling city of the dead. I cannot really describe the sounds that come from across the river, especially at night. My worst childhood fears given "life". I put life in quotes because the sounds that I am hearing right now are hardly the sounds of the living. Ben hides under the covers when it starts, trying to drown out the guttural moaning that echoes from Manhattan. But his nightmares, like my own, mean that even sleep is not an escape from reality any more. In some ways, sleep is worse than awake. At least with awake there is never that moment when you emerge from the world inside your head and go, "Phew, that was just a bad dream," only to realize it's not.


Saturday, May 27, 2017

I'm too depressed to write anything today. Maybe tomorrow. Or maybe never again. Maybe I've had it. Maybe writing in this diary is stupid and I'm sick of stupid. The world is full of stupid. That sums it up. It's a stupid world filled with stupid people hiding from stupid zombies. I refuse to continue adding to the stupidity.


## Tuesday, May 30, 2017

Wow - just read Saturday's entry again. Boy, was I angry and sad when I wrote that. I don't feel so angry or sad anymore. With that said, let me get back to the events outside my own head. It's been pretty crazy these last few days. The barricade along Observer Highway was almost penetrated and then a boat filled with new arrivals drifted across the Hudson from New York, the first in weeks - five men, three women, two children, an infant, a dog, and a cat. It was wonderful. To know that there are still survivors in the city, that my father and uncle could be there - alive - and might somehow find a way to reach us. We all felt kind of hopeful. But hope doesn't last long anymore. Mom says that's how life always was, only the stakes are higher now.

I suppose I should write first about the zombie infiltration along Observer Highway. I'm guessing that whoever reads this is far, far in the future and I've been dead for a long time. I know I promised I wouldn't die, but I am also not stupid, despite Saturday's entry. So I'm going to explain everything in detail. Set the stage, so to speak, for whoever comes next and wants to understand what life was like for us.

It was Memorial Day. I was in the third tower along Observer with Jason, Kahil and Serena. The four of us - all former classmates - were taking the noon to six shift. Serena had a set of the binoculars. It was around 4:00 p.m. and quiet. Suddenly, she yelled, "Incoming zom." Out of nowhere, fifty or more of them were below us, a mangled, twisted pack of undead trying to climb the barricade, flies everywhere, a swarm following a swarm. You don't want to shoot zom if you don't have to because that just calls more of them to your location. Kahil signaled the other towers with a loud whistle and called for reinforcements. Within minutes twenty sharp shooters were there with rifles. This time they had no choice but to start shooting.

The sharp shooters took the zom out one by one with a single shot to the head as they tried to pour through a break in the barricade. Two of the zom were women in burqas - there was a large Muslim population in Jersey City before the outbreak - and though their messed up faces were exposed where their veils had been ripped away, the rest of their bodies were still covered with those thick blue garments, including wherever they each had been bit. It was kind of crazy how they managed to remain mostly covered as they moved with the rest of the pack. Once the last zom was put down, the barricade was quickly repaired and reinforced with sandbags, bricks, scrap metal, and pieces of lumber and trashed furniture, while we continued to watch the horizon for more incoming. The flies lasted long after the last zombie was "killed". Gross, I know.

The zombie scouts were formed immediately after the barricades went up and Hoboken was sealed off from the world. I think it was Hoboken's experience during Hurricane Sandy in 2012 - when I was still just a kid - that made the town vow it would never again be caught off guard. We were flooded with water containing oil, gas, chemicals, bacteria, and debris during that long ago Halloween week. We were not going to be flooded with zombies this time around. I think we were smarter than we would have been in how we faced the zom because of Sandy.

Right away, the City Council passed a decree giving authority to the scouts to monitor the no man's land on the other side since the adults of the town had to direct their attention to other areas of group survival, like food, water, housing, and security. I heard someone say the other day that the Hoboken Internal Security Force now has 5,000 police officers, all volunteers, since no one gets issued paychecks for anything in our new world. The idea of an ATM or online banking is just an old dream. The police officers are needed to make sure Hoboken doesn't cave in on itself. The population has no where to go, and fear and hopelessness are all over the place. We need to be protected from the zom but we also need to be protected from ourselves. The towers were constructed along the barricades the first week we withdrew from the world, and kids were recruited, age twelve to sixteen, to guard the town. We rotate working with pretty much the same group of scouts during all our shifts so that trust and familiarity is built. That is unbelievably important for good zombie scouting. We're a team when we're up there in the tower.

The boat arrival was a much better experience I want to share with you. I was walking along the promenade with Mom and Ben, carrying home supplies from the food coop set up on the campus of Stevens Institute of Technology, when one of the women standing watch along the Hudson yelled out that a boat was approaching. One or two zom have managed to cross over on pieces of debris. Most, though, seem to get stuck in the current and eventually wash out to sea. But the bigger threat from the beginning have been boats, large and small, that drift across filled with zom. Maybe the boats originally held healthy survivors until a dead person reanimated as a zombie among the crowd - that must be a hellish thing to experience - or maybe the zom just wandered onto the boats on the other side and stumbled around deck looking for flesh until the boats began to drift. Either way, no boat can be allowed to dock until we know what's aboard.

As this particular boat neared Hoboken, we could see two men waiving a white bed sheet like a flag of surrender. That is definitely not the actions of your typical zom. We halted in our tracks as Mom dropped her bag of canned goods and screamed, "They're alive!" The three of us rushed to the edge of the pier while the boat approached. The people on board looked as bad as you could imagine. The two kids, a boy and a girl, were skin and bones. The three women cried, realizing they had reached safety. Ben said excitedly, "They've got a dog! And a cat!"

Once on dry land, one of the men explained that they had all been hiding in an apartment just a block from the Greenwich Village waterfront, but it had taken them all these months to plan their escape. They said others were still alive and uninfected in the West Village, though how many they had no idea, and they were clueless about the rest of the city. Four members of the WDC (Welcome and Debriefing Committee) set to work helping the survivors. There is a whole system in place for when healthy people reach us. While the WDC got busy, Mom grabbed Ben and me, held us tight against her, and said, "Boys, I know your father is alive." Mom was happy for the rest of the day and night, staring out the window until almost the next morning, just looking at the dark city across the water, every now and then saying Dad's name loud enough for us to hear - "Ted."

## Wednesday, May 31, 2017

I've been thinking all day about that girl I "killed", the one that got me writing this diary in the first place. It's hard for me to say to myself, "She was a zom. End of story." She seemed like she had been about my age when she crossed over from life to that. Her hair was a bloody rats' nest, pulled out from the skull in whole clumps, and her rotting skin hung off her face at her cheekbones. But I could tell in the few seconds I looked at her that she had once been blond and pretty. She was the kind of girl Jason always got a crush on and constantly talked about until he drove me crazy and I had to tell him to shut up. I'll always feel as if I killed her. I'll never get over that. I know it. And there is nothing I can do but live with the shame and guilt. Live with it until I die with it. Maybe I'll see her in the next life, in heaven, and she'll tell me it's OK. She'll tell me that she forgives me for continuing to smash her brains all over the pavement, even after I knew I had knocked the "zom-ness" out of her. I hope wherever she is now, that she is back to what she was like before she was attacked and bit. I hope she knows I did what I did only to save Jason. I hope she knows how sorry I am for what happened to her and everyone else who now roams aimlessly on the other side of the barricades.

*Thursday, June 1, 2017*

Another month has passed in the Democratic People's Republic of Hoboken. That's what Serena calls it. I guess I should explain how the Democratic People's Republic can exist at all. Hoboken is a one square mile town that is lucky enough to be surrounded by water to the east, train tracks and warehouses all around, and a mountain with cliffs holding Jersey City Heights to the west. That water was a curse during Sandy, but it saved us this time. As soon as there were signs of a zombie outbreak in America, the town got organized and began to build the barricades. The first sandbags and bricks were laid an hour after Passenger Zero landed at Kennedy. From the start of all this zom insanity, everyone knew deep down it was eventually coming here, too. And everyone old enough - who was living in town in October 2012 - never again wanted to see Hoboken destroyed by events outside its control.

The population of Hoboken in January 2017 was 44,629. The City Council right away passed a decree that all life-sustaining property - such as food, water, generators, fuel - was communal property that would be distributed equally among the population. Most people willingly agreed. When the population swelled to 100,000 due to the arrival of refugees the decree was vital for everyone's survival. When the population topped 250,000 it was essential.

Mr. Rosen, a very old man who lives in our building on the tenth floor and is a survivor of the Warsaw Ghetto during World War II, said that he never thought he would live to see another place as packed tight with people, starving and desperate, as there now exists in Hoboken. But because of both the adults and the kids in this town, we figured it out and made it work. We're still here. Every inch of earth, from parks to baseball diamonds to community gardens, is now land given over for growing food to be shared by everyone who has found safety within the barricades of the Democratic People's Republic of Hoboken.

## Sunday, June 4, 2017

Today was a terrible, awful day. One of the worst days yet. None of us who were on scout duty along Observer Highway this afternoon will ever get over what we saw. A large pack of zom approached the barricade around 3:00 p.m., initially in groups of three and four, then in groups of twenty and thirty. They were growling and clawing the air like they always do, looking up at us looking down at them, hungry to devour every last resident of Hoboken.

In the lookout tower immediately to the west were four of my old school friends - Henry, Veronica, Zach, and Maya. As we scanned the crowd below for signs of penetration of the barricade, Maya let out a scream. She spotted her dad in the zombie horde. He was a policeman in Jersey City on duty when everything went to pieces and Hoboken sealed itself off from the world. Like my father, he never returned home to his family. Henry, Zach and Veronica had to physically restrain Maya. She was yelling at the top of her lungs that she wanted to throw herself out of the tower into the pack of zom. She wanted to go to her father. Serena, Jason, Kahil, and I could hear Maya, even over the increasing roar of the zom, who appeared agitated and excited by Maya's screams. All these hours later alone in my room writing, I can still hear her screaming.

When my eye caught sight of Officer Sanchez in his blood-soaked uniform, his right arm missing below his tattooed bicep, just tendons and flesh and the other gross stuff that make up our insides dangling there, I could tell his attention was also drawn to his daughter's screams. Then, just like that, something else got his attention and he turned away. I don't think Maya will ever be able to serve scout duty again. Who can blame her? Poor Maya! If it had been my dad who appeared on the horizon with a pack of zom, I doubt I would ever recover from it. I suppose that could happen one day if he is now a zombie and manages to make his way through the Holland Tunnel to New Jersey. I could spot him in the crowd. Just another mindless zom. Looking up at me on the barricade not as his son but as something to bite, something to rip to shreds without a second thought. Without any thought. Please God, don't let that happen. Ever.

Monday, June 5, 2017

On Saturday, July 15, 1944, Anne Frank, from her prison in that attic in Amsterdam, wrote in her diary that she was surprised she hadn't let go of all her hopes and ideals. The Nazis had invaded the Netherlands and in the process of trampling over Dutch soil they had also trampled over everything important to Anne. But she refused to give up and surrender to the Nazis in any way. She held to her ideals despite everything that was happening around her. Anne believed that people were still good at heart, which I think is an amazing thing considering what was happening to her and her family and friends. She knew that the minute she let go of that thought, everything would come crumbling down inside her. If she concentrated too much on the suffering and death, she would be done for. Europe was becoming a wilderness. The storm clouds had gathered and they would remain hanging in the sky over Amsterdam and the rest of Europe for a long time. But when she looked up at that same sky, Anne truly believed that the storm would pass, that the persecution and murder of the Jews would end, and that peace and tranquility (her two words) would one day return.

Please don't think I'm some kind of weirdo dork of a kid, walking around with famous dead people's diaries memorized in my head. Though if I was that kind of kid, this section from Anne Frank's diary would be exactly what I would memorize. The truth is that Serena goes everywhere with a copy of the *The Definitive Edition of The Diary of a Young Girl: Anne Frank* in her knapsack. I read the entry from July 15, 1944 the other day, and I think it says it all about where we find ourselves at this moment in time. By the way, Serena is keeping a diary, too, and sometimes when we're not on scout duty we sit together and write. Those moments with her, the both of us silent together and writing, are the best moments I know anymore.

Now, I want to be clear about one thing. Yeah, I live in the midst of a zombie apocalypse. But I'm not hiding in a secret annex above a spice factory waiting for the Nazis to show up and cart me off to Auschwitz with my family to be gassed. Though, I think actually Anne Frank died of typhus at Bergen-Belsen along with her sister Margot. I make that correction only because I want to be accurate about all things.

Anyway, as I was saying, I get to go outside and feel the sunshine on my face and know the zom aren't trying to kill me because they think I'm subhuman and they're the master race. I have a fighting chance with them. Living in a world where everyone wants to kill you because of who you are and what you are must be so much worse than living in a world where wild animals prowl the city gates trying to find dinner. And that's basically what we have here.

Anne sat trapped in that attic looking out at a chestnut tree trying to make sense of the world, trying to grow up with insanity all around her, hoping to get just one more day out of life. There are similarities. I think I can understand a little bit what she went through, but I am not saying that I am suffering like she suffered. I know the difference. I'm not an asshole. There goes that cursing thing again.

Like Anne, I want this diary to one day be published. If it were just for me and my eyes only, I would be dropping the f-bomb every other sentence, because let's face it, this is one f-ed up world right now. . . .

But if I write this diary believing that it will one day be published, doesn't that mean that I am assuming there will be a future where people publish and read books? And isn't that the real sign that I live with a sense of hope? That like Anne, I believe this nightmare will be over. And, like Anne, that I believe peace and tranquility will return. One day they will find a cure. Whether virus or bacteria or extraterrestrial parasite, someone somewhere someday will figure out how to stop this. That, or the zom will all rot to the point where they can't threaten anyone. Back to ash and dust and bits of bone. Either way, peace and tranquility will return.

## Tuesday, June 6, 2017

I had a dream about that girl again last night, the one I "killed", or rather didn't kill, but stopped from killing Jason. She didn't look the way she did when we met her. She was pretty and alive and standing in front of a Christmas tree, probably her family's Christmas tree from this past December, back when people all over the world stood with each other beside Christmas trees and Hanukkah menorahs with no idea of what was just around the corner. The girl smiled at me and reached out her hand, which was glowing all halo-y with a really bright light that moved up her arm and spread around her entire body and head. She wasn't just that pretty zombie girl I "killed". She was beautiful. She spoke to me without opening her mouth, without making sound. By telepathy, she told me that she knew I had to do what I did.

She also told me that there was a little bit, the tiniest bit, of the old "her" still left in the zom-girl she had become, and she didn't want to exist like that, possibly for an eternity, or at least until her flesh completely rotted away and her bones turned to dust. I had freed her and she thanked me and said - again without sound - "next world is a much better place." I woke up from that dream feeling calm, which never happens with dreams any more, not for any of us. That was the best dream I ever had, and I'm so grateful to the girl for visiting me that way. Because I believe she did visit me. I believe that dream was a real experience. Crazy, man, for sure. But also really kind of hopeful. It doesn't just end with all this zombie insanity for any of us. There is life after death. Or, I should say, there is life after zom.

## Thursday, June 8, 2017

The common theory is that once one becomes a zombie all human emotion, conscience and awareness is gone. They've supposedly lost that inner sense of what's right and what's wrong. But I don't know if that's completely true. This morning I was working an early shift in the lookout tower with Kahil and a strange girl named Miranda, who I didn't know before all this began. Zombie scout shifts have been reduced to three people for four hours instead of four people for six hours. It's better. Much easier to keep alert for the shorter period of time. And if there is one thing that is important during scout duty, it is staying alert.

Miranda and her mother were among the early refugees who reached us from Manhattan. I say she is strange because she always talks about the zom like she sort of cares about them. We all feel sorry for who they once were. Miranda feels sorry for them as they are now. It doesn't affect her ability to be a good zombie scout. She can spot them coming a mile away. But Miranda somehow still sees the humanness in them. Today, I understood why she might be right.

Every now and then from the crow's nest (just a fancy name for a lookout tower that I thought I'd try out), we see a sole zom wandering around the other side of the barricade. They seem to feed off each other - no pun intended - when they're in groups. That's when the violent, frantic frenzy begins, and they do crazy things just for the sake of a potential piece of living flesh. When they're alone they seem like they have thoughts and are actually a little depressed. What I saw today amazed me and Kahil, and made Miranda say, "See, there is something still kind of human in them."

A female zom was pushing a baby carriage on the other side of the barricade, though not with the greatest care or ease. Inside the carriage was an intertwined mess of three or four of the youngest zom any of us have seen yet. Small children tend not to get bit once or twice, crawl away and die somewhere, and rise up as the undead. Most children - certainly babies and toddlers - seem to get devoured on the spot by the zom who kill them, with nothing left of them to walk again and join the hordes. This scene was different.

We took turns with the binoculars watching this zom as she pushed her carriage filled with what appeared to be growling, rabid raccoons. There was no doubt these were zombie kids, no more than a couple years old when they died. Was this their mother? Who knew. Was she in some way protecting them? We could not even begin to figure out what had happened and what, if anything, was motivating her to continue to push that carriage along the other side of the barricade. All I could do was agree with Miranda when she said it. "See, there is something still kind of human in them." I've stopped thinking Miranda is so strange after that incident.

Friday, June 9, 2017

It's late, way past 11:00 p.m., but there is an incredible full moon tonight. I can almost make out through the telescope

Uncle Matt gave us for Christmas the Moonbase Lunar Colony they began constructing last year. The moon tonight is huge and bright and hangs in the sky over New York City, almost as if it's perched on top of the tallest skyscrapers, just to the north of the eerily dark Empire State Building. There's a lot I've had to accept as changed forever, but I will never get used to looking at the Empire State Building and the rest of the skyline unlit.

The moon is thankfully bright enough for me to write at this hour with no candle or flashlight, which is important because such essentials cannot be wasted on my diary. Since air conditioning is no more, the windows have to remain open at night or else we'll all suffocate in the intense heat. I can hear the howling now from across the river. It echoes through the canyons of Manhattan, bouncing against the buildings and across the Hudson. There is not a shred of Miranda's humanness in the sound they make at night. It's like werewolves mixed with torture victims mixed with people who died and found out there really is a hell.

Ben is under the covers despite the heat. He is terrified by the howling and groaning. I try to assure him that we're safe and that I'm certain Dad and Uncle Matt are hiding somewhere safe as well. But he's only eight years old, still such a kid. He doesn't deserve to have this happen to him now. Eight to fourteen are the best years of childhood. I had those years. Ben never will and that breaks my heart. His father is missing, maybe dead. His mother is so sad and depressed with no opportunity for a psychiatrist to help her. He only has me. I have to raise Ben. I have to protect Ben. He used to drive me crazy. I even sometimes wished he had never been born. Now he is my child. Not just my brother, but my son, too.

I'm going to stop writing now so I can crawl in bed with him and hold him, try to get him to go to sleep. I'll tell him a story about the moon, how we'll build a shuttle rocket and make our way to the lunar colony, where there are no zombies and life can begin again. We'll grow old on the moon together, Ben and I, and it will be a good life. You'll see.

## Saturday, June 10, 2017

I've decided to list the things I miss most. In no specific order: music, television (there was supposed to be a new season of *Doctor Who* on BBC America in April), ice cream (cherry vanilla, chocolate, and Ben & Jerry's cake batter), pizza (pepperoni, meatball and black olive was my favorite), my father, school (yes, school!), especially Mr. Chupka (the Chupkanator), my English teacher, who is by far the best teacher I've ever had and this totally cool guy, the internet, iCards, iPods, iBrains, my mother the way she was before all this happened, Facebook2, airplanes flying above, texting, eboarding, skateboarding, Uncle Matt and Tolstoy, my friend Ryan who was in Florida when everything went down, hamburgers, onion rings, unlimited electricity, running water, hot showers, McDonald's, Chinese takeout, going to the movies, the Hudson River filled with ferries, ships, and hydrofoils, New York City lit up at night (especially the Empire State Building), springtime when it meant the rebirth of life. I miss all of it. And a thousand things more.

## Sunday, June 11, 2017

I wonder if the President is alive somewhere. Another unfortunate, truly sucky result of the zombie outbreak is that we barely got to experience a few weeks of the first female American President. That's right, the first woman President (and the good one, not the other dreaded possibility despised by both my parents and Uncle Matt) was sworn in like every past American President on January 20th, just as the eastern hemisphere was beginning its domino collapse. She was on TV that first night of her presidency, assuring the country we would find a way to "fight the scourge and survive together as a united nation." Her face and voice were a constant in our lives those first weeks, and then she was gone, along with everything else television and the internet brought into our homes. Crazy, man.

We had a great leader, who maybe is still leading us somehow, somewhere. But it is pretty clear we are on our own. Hoboken is the entire world right now for us. Whatever else might exist out there beyond the barricades doesn't matter. If this town collapses it could mean the end of civilization. That is what is at stake here. We don't say it to each other every day, but we all think it. It's the unsaid thing behind every word and action. A responsibility my friends and I do not take lightly as we fulfill our duty - our sacred duty - as zombie scouts protecting not just Hoboken, but all of human civilization.

## Tuesday, June 13, 2017

The heatwave continues. There wasn't much winter this year but there is sure going to be summer. A summer of flies and walking corpses. When I was a kid, people talked about global warming all the time. I don't think anyone cares one bit about global warming anymore, and clearly we're seeing its effects. There were three main things everyone feared just a few years ago during my childhood: 1. Global warming and another hurricane; 2. Al Qaeda terrorists and their copycat wannabes (both cyber terrorists and the old fashioned bombing kind, like the thugs who blew up those pizzerias and coffee shops in Brooklyn and Manhattan in 2015) and; 3. Bed bugs. Frankly, once the economy began to improve in 2013 after the Great Recession, the explosion of bed bugs became our main preoccupation.

Every choice my mother made about where we went and what we brought into the apartment was controlled by bed bugs and her careful analysis of whether a particular thing might introduce them into our home. It was a little OCD on her part, and we used to laugh at her about it. But I'll hand it to my mother. Never once did a bed bug cross our doorstep, despite their being everywhere in society. Looking back, our war with the bed bugs was preparation for what would come next. They were micro-zombies and we constantly had to be on watch in our fight against them or else they would overwhelm us. We could not peacefully co-exist together. It was either us or them. My mother made sure we won when it came to the bed bugs. Now it's my job to make sure we win when it comes to the zom. I owe my mother at least that.

## Thursday, June 15, 2017

Starting next week I'm taking lessons at the shooting range at Stevens Tech. Once you turn fourteen, a zombie scout can train as a sharp shooter. But, my mother wouldn't agree until this morning. I suppose I could have done it anyway without her permission. Except she seems so beaten down lately. I figured if the idea of me shooting zom upset her that much, I'd let it go for the time being until I could win her over. My mother turned a corner today, however, and I think it was because of Mr. Rosen's visit last night.

He came down to our apartment with two cans of baked beans and some fresh herbs from his window sill garden and turned those beans and herbs into a feast. Over dinner he told us more about his childhood. About the Warsaw Ghetto. And about a place called Treblinka where he ended up. He kept apologizing, saying he didn't mean to upset us with sad stories from the past, when he should be telling us nice stories to cheer us up. But I was OK with the sad stories. Mom and Ben were, too. And it seemed to help Mr. Rosen - he's such a kind, old man - to clear his mind of what he suffered through as a boy.

He was born in 1927 - which makes him ninety now and the oldest person I know by a long shot - in the Polish village of Gora Kalwaria on the Vistula River. His family was super Orthodox, like the Jewish people we used to see in midtown when we went to the city on Sunday afternoons. There is a specific term for those super Orthodox Jewish people (I think it begins with "H"), but I can't recall it. I'm lucky I remember "Gora Kalwaria" and all the dates and names from Mr. Rosen's story. Ben tried to remember the word after Mr. Rosen left and referred to them as "Subatomic" Jews. But I know that's not right. Wait, it's coming to me - "Hasidic". That's the term.

Mr. Rosen used the word "idyllic" to describe his child-hood. As a small boy he would run along the banks of the

Vistula playing with his brothers and sisters (he had three of each). He said he has a soft spot in his heart for life along a river and that is what drew him to our building, where he has a tiny balcony to sit out on that overlooks the Hudson. He said he still misses the Vistula, and you could hear the missing of it in his voice as he talked.

The Nazis invaded Poland on September 1, 1939. By October 6, 1939, Poland had been conquered and divided between Germany and the old Soviet Union. Mr. Rosen said everything changed from that point on. At first, the Jews of Gora Kalwaria were rounded up and forced into a small ghetto that was part of Gora Kalwaria. As terrible as that was for them, things got so much worse. In July of 1942 they were rounded up again and forced into cattle cars. They ended up in the Warsaw Ghetto - the largest ghetto in Europe - where over 400,000 lived in an area about 1.3 square miles in size. At the moment, we have about 250,000 (some say we're close to 300,000) people living in the one square mile that makes up Hoboken, just to put their situation and our situation in perspective.

By the time Mr. Rosen and his family and the other Jews of Gora Kalwaria arrived in Warsaw, the Ghetto had been sealed off from the rest of the city for twenty months, and starvation and disease were on every street, around every corner. Mr. Rosen said he sees the early signs of this hopelessness and collapse in Hoboken, and prays every night that there are scientists and doctors somewhere working on a solution to the zombie pandemic (his word, but a cool one that I am going to start using).

During the summer of 1942, just after Mr. Rosen arrived with his family, the Nazis began to liquidate the Warsaw Ghetto. "Liquidate" is a word I never knew until last night. Now that I know what it means, I think it is the worst word I've ever heard. Mr. Rosen remembers that it was a Friday morning in early September of 1942. He was fifteen at the time, the oldest of his family except for his sister Eva. The Germans cordoned off the city block where Mr. Rosen lived with his parents and siblings. His family was forced into the street with all their neighbors. The Nazis marched them to a freight yard where they waited in the hot sun all day with 5,000 other people until the cattle cars arrived again.

With 150 people packed into each car, Mr. Rosen said that was the most frightened he has ever been in his life, as well as the most thirsty. He told us about the awful trip from Warsaw to Treblinka. It hurts me just to think about it. Every type of person - every size and age and physical condition - were pushed against each other without any room to sit or turn. Mostly in the dark with light creeping now and then through the cracks, the 149 other people in the boxcar with Mr. Rosen cried and prayed and vomited and fainted. And in some cases, died. Mr. Rosen said the longest cattle car deportation to the camps took eighteen days. From Corfu, a Greek island in the Ionian Sea. When the train arrived at

Auschwitz and the doors were opened, no one inside was alive. Just corpses spilled out onto the tracks.

Very few people from Mr. Rosen's transport who survived the trip were not immediately gassed. Maybe twenty, including Mr. Rosen and his thirteen year old brother Yaacov (my name, Jack, in Hebrew). A barber who knew them from Gora Kalwaria had them pulled out of line, claiming they used to work for him. This wasn't true, but the man wanted to save them. Mr. Rosen's parents were sent to the gas chamber right away, as was Eva (16), Rachel (12), Noam (9), Giza (8), and Aaron (5).

For the rest of his time in Treblinka, Mr. Rosen and his brother worked along side the barber from Gora Kalwaria - his name was Hershel - cutting the hair off women and girls before they were sent to the gas chamber. The women filed in one after another and sat on a stool naked as Mr. Rosen cut their hair. He couldn't bring himself to look directly at them. He constantly turned his eyes away from their breasts as the women tried to cover themselves with their arms. He felt so ashamed of himself for doing what he did to survive. That is definitely worse than this. That is unspeakably worse than this. Life amidst the zom doesn't compare with what Mr. Rosen and his brother experienced when they were my age. I don't take comfort in that. I just admit it, both to myself and to all of you.

There is one last part to Mr. Rosen's story. On August 2, 1943, the inmates at Treblinka staged an uprising with stolen weapons, and about 600 escaped into the woods. Mr. Rosen said he and Yaacov ran as fast as they could after making it through a hole in the barbed wire fence. But Yaacov was shot in the back as they ran. Mr. Rosen dragged him behind some thick bushes and Yaacov died in his arms. Before he died, Yaacov begged Mr. Rosen to continue running, to save himself. No surprise to me that Mr. Rosen could not and would not leave his brother to die alone in the woods. I would never have left Ben. I never will leave Ben. Mr. Rosen survived the remainder of the war because a Polish Catholic farmer and his wife hid him in a barn.

Poor Mr. Rosen was the only survivor of his family. He married another Holocaust survivor. Her name was Ester, and though they had many years together until Mrs. Rosen died of cancer in 2002, they never had any children. Mrs. Rosen was not able to have a baby because of what the Nazis did to her, because of the experiments and other awful things she endured at Auschwitz. Mr. Rosen said his wife was beautiful and the Nazis were especially brutal to beautiful Jewish women. It's so beyond twisted and messed up that people, not zombies, did what they did to other people in Europe seventy-five years ago.

The Nazis were worse than the zom, which is saying a lot. The zom don't know what they're doing. The Nazis knew what they were doing. The Nazis made choices. They knew they were murdering women and children and old people. Cramming them into gas chambers so tight those poor people didn't even have room to fall over as they fought for their last breath. Mr. Rosen told us about it. He told us everything about it. Mr. Rosen told us how the trains from Warsaw would pull into Treblinka Station, but only a handful of boxcars could be emptied at a time. The other cars would sit and wait, sometimes for hours. Often half the occupants of each car were dead upon arrival. From heat and starvation and suicide and thirst.

Several thousand people would be stripped of their clothes and possessions and hair, and driven naked - half-mad at that point after all they had suffered - by German and Ukrainian guards through a funnel surrounded by barbed wire and interwoven twigs and branches. The men would be gassed first. The women and children knew what was happening by the sounds of the men slowly dying. The women would scream and pray and comfort their children and involuntarily empty their bowels (I think that's the polite way to put it). It took thirty minutes or more to die in the carbon monoxide gas they used at Treblinka. The human race just might deserve the zom. For Treblinka alone, if for nothing else. Poor, Mr. Rosen. We are all he has left in the world.

*Sunday, June 18, 2017*

I walked along Washington Street today and saw the signs of what Mr. Rosen was talking about the other night. People are crowded together everywhere. In fact, Mr. Rosen got a notice yesterday that he either has to give up his apartment or take in refugees. Mom insisted that he move in with us, and he agreed. On Washington and all the side streets, entire families are living in tents and makeshift structures. Since there is little electricity (only what we can get from generators) and water is rationed (every rooftop is covered with barrels and pans to catch the rain), most apartments are very hot and windows remain open all the time.

The residents of Hoboken live outside as much as possible, and this new form of street life and the constant interaction between people has tempers rising with fights multiplying. You can feel the collapse of society - what little there is left of civilized society - hanging in the air. Maybe months, if not weeks away. Eventually, something has got to give. And I'm not talking about the barricades that keep out the zom. I think some people are truly going insane. Trust me, you can't live the way we do for long and not have it get to you.

*Friday, June 23, 2017*

Mr. Rosen moved in with us today. He sleeps in the spare bedroom. Mom has definitely cheered up with a new person in our home. Mr. Rosen seems to understand Mom and feel deeply for her suffering. He told me the other day that she reminds him of his own mother, who became very depressed when his family was deported to Warsaw. I worry about Mom and sometimes become angry with her for putting so much on my shoulders. Mr. Rosen says that it's always easier for young people to adapt to difficult circumstances and continue fighting. The older a person is when trouble comes, the harder it is for them to let go of the past. I think that Hoboken would have fallen months ago if it wasn't for its young people.

It's funny, the things adults say to each other. I wonder if they truly mean most of what comes out of their mouths. I was walking up the stairs of our building behind two women earlier today. The elevators stopped working a long time ago. People joke that there's no need to hit a gym anymore to use a StairMaster. As we trudged up the eight flights, one of the women turned to the other and said, "At least I haven't gotten a credit card bill since December." The other woman replied, "Yeah, I hear ya'. Thanks zom! No more debt to worry about." I suppose they were doing what we all do every day here in Hoboken, trying to find a way to cope with the hugeness of our situation, sometimes with humor. Sarcasm does help. It just sounded strange to hear someone thank the zom for anything. I mean, how much credit card debt exactly could they have had to prefer a zombie apocalypse over getting a Visa or American Express bill in the mail? Crazy, man.

## Saturday, June 24, 2017

This afternoon I watched Ben and Mr. Rosen playing cards on the window sill. Mr. Rosen was sitting in my dad's leather chair. Ben was standing, that way eight-year-olds stand with their legs crossed, leaning on the sill with his left arm and holding his cards close. The light streamed in on the both of them as Mr. Rosen taught my brother the rules of poker. I stood by the entrance to the kitchen, watching from across the living room. It was nice. It was normal. Mr. Rosen is good for all of us. I think we'll look back on these days and see that without him coming to live with us we would have had a much more difficult time.

## Tuesday, June 27, 2017

My sharp shooting lessons continue. Jason and Serena are learning to shoot with me. Kahil won't be fourteen until August so he doesn't qualify yet. Miranda says she refuses to ever shoot a gun. She would have been a real hippie back in the 1960s, from what I know of that era. I don't enjoy firing a gun, but I think it is a necessity to learn given the world in which we find ourselves. Thankfully, Hoboken has plenty of ammo after a dozen men raided a deserted navy battleship back in April that was docked across the river.

As everyone knows, shooting zom in the head from a distance is the safest way to put them down. Everyone, that is, except Miranda, who believes the zom are not just the dead walking again with no hope of ever being anything else. She thinks a cure is on the way and they can all be saved, returned back to who they once were. I think this is a noble belief that is also extremely dangerous. Maybe the zom are completely dead, maybe not. No one knows if their souls have departed their bodies for heaven or not. Should they still be considered part of the human species? Sometimes I see them as us but different. When they come at you with teeth bared and arms flailing, however, they are most definitely coming in for the kill. And you either end up as dinner, or worse, one of them. I won't hesitate to shoot a thousand of them if I have to. For sure. End of story.


*Thursday, June 29, 2017*

I was down by the water with Ben today, taking Mr. Rosen for a walk. I don't mean to make it sound like he's a dog or anything. But at ninety years old it's difficult for him to get around on his own, especially up and down the stairs of our building. As we walked, suddenly the river guards began whistling and shouting. Someone was in the Hudson trying to make their way across. The person was swimming, doing their best to stay above the water as they became obviously more exhausted. I had my binoculars with me - a nice, old-time pair from the 1940s that Mr. Rosen found and gave to me when he moved out of his apartment. I looked across the river at the other shore. Fifty, maybe a hundred zom, were going nuts on the other side, probably having chased this poor person to the water's edge. They seem afraid of water - these zombies - or at least confused by it, so they generally don't jump in. One more piece of critical information to keep in mind when you live in a world overrun by them.

I couldn't tell if the person in the water was a man or a woman, but it was clear to me they were having trouble fighting for each stroke. Two of the river guards set out in a small boat and reached the person just in time. When they got to Hoboken's shore, we realized it was a woman. Mr. Rosen, Ben and I walked to the boat and learned that her name is Lily. Lily Kramer. She is 27 years old and apparently had survived alone in the city for a long time.

Through gasping breath, Lily told us that while out scavenging for something to eat today she encountered this massive pack of zom, who tore after her like hungry seagulls diving for discarded food at the beach. They were vicious, determined and fast. She ran several blocks to the water, intending to jump in and drown herself. Once in the water, she realized she still had some strength left and began to swim toward New Jersey. Lily didn't know help was waiting for her on the other side. She just swam out of instinct and she made it. One more refugee for the Democratic People's Republic of Hoboken.

## Sunday, July 2, 2017

Everyone who has a large apartment like ours has been told they must take in additional refugees. The W Hotel next door to our building has already been filled two times over. It was once a pretty swanky, posh place. Now it looks more like the Projects on the west side of town, teeming with kids and laundry hanging off the balconies. Due to the overcrowding, in addition to Mr. Rosen we have opened our door to Lily Kramer. Mr. Rosen asked Mom if it would be OK with her and then extended the invitation to Lily. I would be leaving out a critical piece of information if I did not say that Lily is beautiful. My friends would call her extremely hot. Mom said that she thought Lily looked like a younger Natalie Portman. Yes, that's it. Natalie Portman (circa *V for Vendetta* 2006, before they shaved her character's head) is definitely who would play Lily in the movie version of this nightmare. You know, I wonder if Natalie Portman is now a zombie? Kind of weird. All the beautiful people, all the celebrities, all the professional athletes and rock stars are just as likely to now be roaming America amongst the zom as any truck driver or homeless person or fourteen year old kid. Crazy, man, for sure!

With each new person added to our home, Mom seems to cheer up a little more. She still has her dark days, though, where she can't speak or get out of bed. Mr. Rosen is very good at nursing her during these bad days, and I will always be grateful to him for that because I don't think I could have done it alone with everything else I have to do. Like be sure we have sufficient food and water, care for Ben, force him to continue with his studies, work my double shift on the barricade.

We set up a sleeping nook for Lily by moving an armoire and skillfully arranging two Japanese screens. Her first night with us Lily didn't stop talking once. She kept apologizing, explaining that she had been alone since her boyfriend Doug went out one day in early April to search for food and never returned to their hiding place. She said that there are still people alive in Manhattan who live like rats in attics, sewers and basements. They encounter each other now and then, and some have established small makeshift communities, though nothing on the scale of Hoboken. She heard of one on the hill above the United Nations overlooking the East River in a neighborhood called Tudor City, but was never able to get there. Nightfall is when the zom come out in droves, which we know from here. They wander around in daylight as well, though much more sluggish for some reason than at night. Lily was surprised to be ambushed by them the way she was since it was mid afternoon and she didn't think they could run so fast in the heat and light of day.

The strangest and most frightening story Lily told us that first night involved a trek through the subway tunnels when Doug was still with her. They were trying to get home after an expedition downtown to scavenge for supplies. In the darkness of a tunnel they came upon a train stuck between stations. Doug shined his flashlight on the last car and saw that it was filled with zom, fifty or so trapped inside climbing over each other and clawing at the blood soaked windows. They had probably been in there like that for at least two months. Doug shined the flashlight forward onto the next car and it was empty, though the windows were equally soaked with blood and the back door of the car was slid open. Lily and Doug ran in the opposite direction, convinced they heard the howling of zom echoing through the tunnel, and eventually made their way to another tunnel that led them home. I wonder if the zom all stumbled on the train together when there was still electricity and the doors opened and closed at a station stop. Or did a bit person fall over dead and reanimate while the train was moving? I can't imagine how awful it must have been for the last people attacked in the car if it happened that way.

Mom insists that Dad and Uncle Matt are in one of those basements or attics, or better yet in Tudor City. My assessment is that Mom always thinks about Dad's fate and where he might be to the point where she starts to doubt what she first told herself, and begins to worry that he's now just one of the horde of zom. She doesn't come right out and say this. She would never give words to the idea of Dad being a zombie. But I know it's where her mind goes and leads her to despair. I say Dad may be alive, though most likely he isn't. With certainty, however, I know that Mom and I and Ben are alive, and our family now includes Mr. Rosen and Lily, too. We are here in Hoboken, on the still spinning Planet Earth during a zombie apocalypse, and there is nothing else we can count on. This is all we can know and we have to deal with where we find ourselves at the moment. Everyone else must be considered zom food. Or zom. If they show up one day on the pier or at the barricade still fully human, then great. Until that happens, they're dead. To think otherwise is a sure path to one's own death sentence.

Wednesday, July 5, 2017

Independence Day yesterday and I spent it like our Revolutionary War forefathers - fighting on the barricades. Past years we were able to watch the annual Macy's fireworks over the Hudson River from our apartment. Not this year. I guess that goes without saying. This 4th of July was the hottest day I can ever remember in my life. So hot that it actually got people talking about global warming again. The flies were out in full force. I was working the sunset shift with Serena and Kahil in the third lookout tower along Observer Highway. The sun was going down but the heat was still unbearable. As I wiped my sweaty face for the upteenth time, I noticed approaching from the southwest the largest pack of zom I've seen yet. We use the word "horde" a lot. This was horde upon horde, at least a thousand, maybe more.

We whistled to the second tower and they whistled to the first tower and the sharp shooters arrived. Serena and I are both now allowed to scout while armed, having completed our sharp shooter training. There was no need to fear attracting other zom with the sound of the shots since every able-bodied zombie in Hudson County seemed to be approaching Hoboken. Serena and I started firing along with the sharp shooters. With this many zom below, penetration of the barricade was far more likely, and that could not be allowed. They were climbing over each other in a frenzy, smelling human flesh on the other side, knowing in whatever way they know things that we were there, wanting us for dinner. It's strange how they won't go after animals, just people. Several wild dogs (I suppose all dogs on the other side of the barricades could now be considered wild) ran along the outside of the pack trying to get their own supper. You see, rotting flesh drops off the zom as they throw themselves around, and the hungry dogs that follow them hoping for a scrap gobble it up like its Purina puppy chow. Pretty gross. But, hey, that's life in 2017 as we know it. Dogs and flies and zom, oh my! Sorry about that.

As Serena and I continued to fire, hitting zom after zom square in the head, the pack began to thin out instead of breaking through the barricade. It appeared that the pile of zom corpses got in the way of those still crazy for food. This morning at sunrise the Zombie Disposal Corp (ZDC) had to exit the safety of Hoboken via the sewer and pile the "bodies" on handcars, pushing the handcars down the track to a lime pit created in a construction site next to the Erie-Lackawanna Train Station. The Observer Highway barricade was constructed to curve along Hudson Place so that the train station is in no man's land. We can't have zom from the city pouring into Hoboken from the PATH train tunnels. A new kind of commuter for 2017.

We have no choice but to dispose of decaying zom corpses in this enormous lime pit. The lime dissolves their flesh along with the odor causing bacteria that fester in the dead. Initially, someone suggested dumping all zom corpses in the Hudson, but it was feared this could cause an ecological disaster since we rely on the fish in that river for food. The ZDC is one of the most difficult jobs in town, but it must be done after a big kill like we had yesterday or else the stench would become unbearable.

When the kill was over, Serena and I struggled to catch our breath. I felt my heart pumping so fast I thought it was going to burst out of my chest, take off, and fly away. The adrenaline rush was amazing, like what taking drugs must be like. Though, who needs drugs if you can experience the real thing. But the dreams I had last night were horrible. This had been less personal than when I "killed" the girl. Still, this zombie scout business is not for the squeamish. Although, can anyone who remains alive have a squeamish bone left in their body? I don't see how.

It's like Planet Earth was invaded by deadly extraterrestrials and we must engage them in battle. Only, the extraterrestrials are us. A twist on *War of the Worlds*. We were here all along lying in wait for ourselves, buried deep in the earth under every major city, biding our time until it was the right moment to rise up and conquer the planet. It was us. It was always us. At every gruesome, nasty point in history it has been us. Crazy, man.


*Thursday, July 6, 2017*

It's as if we live cut off from the rest of humanity, 250,000+ people adrift on a starship sailing through a hostile and alien universe. Every now and then someone from the outside, like Lily, makes their way to us. What we have found is that those who spent time out in the wilderness do not arrive in Hoboken bearing any new information. They know nothing more about what caused the zombie pandemic than us, nor do they understand the ins and outs of this mutation of humanity any more than we do. Within the walls of this town, this mini-metropolis, this place that might be the largest city left in the world, there are increasing philosophical debates about why the zombie pandemic happened now in human history. I guess this is to be expected when people live trapped in one place on top of each other with nothing but time on their hands.

The greatest means of communication we have in town is the weekly newspaper, one page (we don't want to run out of ink) published every Wednesday without fail since early March, printed on an old-fashioned, hand-operated printing press found in the basement of the Hoboken Reporter. It mostly explains security protocol updates and offers survival tips. There are also guest columnists from time to time, including a philosophy professor from Stevens Tech, a rabbi, Father Murphy from Our Lady of Grace, and a medium named Mary Rogers who had a thriving business on Garden Street even before the apocalypse.

Interestingly, Mary Rogers has the same name as a young girl who was found floating in the water off Sybil's Cave in Hoboken in 1841 and nicknamed by the press at the time as "The Beautiful Cigar Girl" because she was employed as a cigar salesgirl before her death. Her body was badly bruised and the mystery of her death was never solved. I know this story because it was included at the beginning of the last column written by our Mary Rogers, who made a little joke that the other Mary Rogers had not yet communicated with her to solve the mystery. The column's main theme concerned the various sessions our Mary has been having with town residents, all of whom are desperate to find out if missing loved ones are already on the other side. And by that I don't mean the other side of the barricades. She explained that not once during any session have souls come through and said that they had crossed over, but their bodies remain here walking with the zom. So, if you believe this sort of thing - which I am not committing to either way at this point - either Miranda is right and zombies retain their souls. Or the dead have no clue that they still walk the Earth. Either way, it really makes you think.

## Sunday, July 9, 2017

A full moon again so I can write tonight. Mom has been happy this week, acting almost motherly toward Lily, who is clearly suffering after her terrifying experiences. When she screams out in the middle of the night, Mom and Mr. Rosen rush to her and calm her down. Mom seems almost to enjoy someone needing her so much. Is it possible that Ben and I have acted as if we don't need her? Maybe that happened at a certain point in all of this. I don't know. All I care about is that Mom has been less depressed since Lily arrived, and the less depressed she is, the better a mother she can be to Ben. And the less, then, that I have to worry about.

It is hot tonight, hotter than Venus or Mercury hot. Luckily, we have an apartment that faces the river and can open our windows for the breeze. It must be stifling and deadly on the blocks west of Washington Street. I hear the wail of zombies now drifting across the Hudson on the night air. From this distance, the sound is more sad than frightening. Or maybe the more we live with the zom the less we despise them. The more they are just something else we have to figure out how to coexist with on the planet.

I have been thinking about the term "reanimated", which I have used in these pages to describe the crossing over from human to zom. I learned that term from the zombie novel, *World War Z*, written by the great Max Brooks. Dad and Uncle Matt were huge zombie movie and book fans, and they loved *World War Z*, which I think was published in 2006. Ironic, one might say, that they watched those movies and read that book partly for entertainment, but maybe also partly because in their subconscious they both knew what was coming.

I think a lot of people sensed for a long time that one day the dead would rise and walk the Earth. It has been part of American folklore since the mid-twentieth century. Eleven years since the publication of *World War Z* and the zombie pandemic is as real as anything that has ever happened in human history. For sure, it is the worst thing to ever happen in human history. Truth is stranger than fiction. But fiction sometimes predicts the truth to come.

One funny, or not so funny, thing I want to add here is that when the movie *World War Z* came out in 2013, Mom wouldn't let Dad take me to see it because she thought I was too young for all the violence in it. In 2013 I was older than Ben is now. It's pretty messed up that at the age of ten I was too young to see fake zombie violence but at eight Ben has to live through it for real. This is definitely a place where I have to say, "Crazy, man!"

## Tuesday, July 11, 2017

Today is Uncle Matt's birthday and I find myself believing that he and my dad are alive somewhere across that river trying to figure a way out and back to us. I know I'm having a sentimental reaction with the date and all. Uncle Matt was such a cool guy. He was a professor of Russian History at NYU (a cat named Tolstoy, I suppose, is a dead giveaway; and, yes, I am aware that I just wrote about him in the past tense). I don't want to think of Dad and Uncle Matt either together or alone in that city, hiding in the sewers or some dark subway tunnel, every moment consumed with staying one foot ahead of the zom. If I could have them both back, if only a boat drifted across the Hudson tomorrow containing Dad, Uncle Matt and Tolstoy, I would be happy beyond anything I can even comprehend at the moment. If they came back to us, I would never in my life require further proof that God exists.

I have written that I know Dad is dead because I am trying to accept something. I fear the worst has happened. When the guttural moaning echoes across the river at night to my bedroom, my father's voice is most likely part of that sound. But at night before I go to sleep, I also pray for Dad and Uncle Matt. I pray that they are safe, and I beg God with every ounce of Catholic school boy left in me to please give me back my father and my uncle. We'll see if God listens any longer to the cries from Planet Earth.

Of course, the zom are part of God's creation, too. Maybe God loves them more than he loves us. Or maybe there simply isn't a God. Life originated with the Big Bang and things continuously evolved until this unfortunate mutation came along. My guess is it's some combination of the two, a little bit of God's grand plan mixed with an unfortunate biological mutation. Ultimately, it doesn't matter. It is what it is what it is. . . . There I go again. I think the term I'm looking for is "fatalism". Unless it's "determinism". I'd google it, but. . . . Wait, I just remembered we have an actual paper dictionary somewhere. I'll look it up later.

Saturday, July 15, 2017

We normally see wild dogs on the other side of the barricade only when zom approach, trailing alongside the pack looking for scraps of food. Though I doubt you need me to explain again that disgusting new evolution in the food chain. Today, however, while I was on morning scout duty with Jason and Miranda, a different kind of dog approached. He was black in color and looked from a distance to be real scrawny, as if he wasn't getting his daily intake from the zombie horde like the others. I write "he" because that's what I first thought he was. Miranda said it was sexist for me to assume the dog was a male. Oh, brother.

When he reached the barricade he was scratching and pawing and sniffing like crazy, trying to dig his way under and into Hoboken. I was afraid that he would succeed in penetrating the barricade, leaving us vulnerable to the sudden appearance of a zom or two. They seem to show up sometimes out of nowhere. I decided to climb down from the tower. With Jason covering me while Miranda continued to scan the horizon for incoming zom, I began to dig from our side to create a small opening for the dog. He was determined to get in as he squeezed his thin body under the barricade, which I quickly resealed with rocks and sandbags.

The dog went nuts upon making it to our side, throwing himself on his back and begging for me to stroke his belly. He was the sweetest dog and while rubbing his underside I realized that Miranda was right and he was in fact a she. Our shift was almost over, so Jason and Miranda shouted down from above that they would be OK for the last few minutes if I wanted to take my new friend home.

There are plenty of pets in Hoboken - dogs and cats and birds and turtles and fish and guinea pigs and hamsters and lizards - and my only fear is that one day the food will run out and our pets may have to be sacrificed. For now, they exist with us in the sanctuary of this town and we care for them as best we can. Many a kid forsakes part of his or her dinner every night for the family pet, despite the protests of parents who insist their children need the nourishment more than an animal.

As I walked with my new friend, I decided she seemed more mutt than purebred. In the sunshine, her dark fur revealed coppery undertones. She was wearing a collar with a tag and her name was Ginger, a good name for her I thought given her coloring. When I got home Mom gasped at the sight of Ginger entering the door behind me, but everyone else took to her right away, especially Ben. When Mom heard how determined Ginger had been to reach us and how she hadn't been traveling with a pack of dogs following the zom, she granted her refugee status and said Ginger could stay. Our family now is me, Ben, Mom, Mr. Rosen, Lily, and Ginger.

Sunday, July 16, 2017

Ginger has breathed new life into our often sad, depressed home. She is grateful for every morsel of food we give her, every pat on the head. She arrived covered with ticks so Mom made Ben and me take her outside and remove all of them before Ginger could return to the apartment. While Ben held her down to calm her, I searched every inch of her fur and with a tweezer removed at least two dozen of the little buggers. It was like hunting minizombies, the bedbugs all over again. There's no end to the parasites on this planet.

The heatwave broke last night, which is the most welcome news Hoboken could imagine other than a cure for the pandemic. With the change in weather, everyone in town is much less cranky. This makes life here so much more pleasant. I've noticed also that people around town have been getting thinner by the day. I can't remember the last time I saw a person I would describe as fat. Some of the kids I see playing on the sidewalks (all of the playgrounds are now used for growing food) look downright malnourished.

Another benefit to the cooler temperatures (and we're only talking low 80s instead of high 90s and above) is that everyone smells less funky. With water rationed to a minimum, daily baths and long, hot showers are a thing of the past. I swear it's debatable at this point who smells more rank, the zom or the citizens of Hoboken. But you get used to the putrid stench of the living. The zom are another story. A drop in temperature doesn't affect their rancid, rotting aroma one bit. With each passing day those roaming the other side of the barricade are more and more decomposed. If you focus too clearly through the binoculars you see the maggots and worms that have hatched and thrive in the eye sockets of the walking dead.

Speaking of *The Walking Dead* - it's funny how that show was such a huge hit a few years back and now I doubt anyone would tune in, if there was still television that is. Actually, I shouldn't say that. Both Max Brooks' *World War Z* and *The Zombie Survival Guide* are much sought after texts in our brave new world. A lot of what we know about dealing with the zom came from this visionary author and others like him, such as the incredible filmmaker George A. Romero (director of *Night of the Living Dead* - the original one).

It always seemed odd to me that in most zombie movies, the characters existed in a world without zombie movies. Like when it started to happen around them they were all, "Oh My God! What's happening? Why are these dead people chasing after us?" Granted, it took us some time to figure it out when the first reports came from Central Asia. But that was just denial, not ignorance. Once we knew the zombie apocalypse was here, those movies and books were the first things we looked at to figure out how to survive. Of course, what we are experiencing is different than any of the fictional accounts. That's to be expected. Our type of "zom-ness" has the ability to flare up immediately in the bit and infected after they die. And they often die in seconds. But it also seems to be able to linger undetected in some for many months, as occurred obviously in Rio de Janero.

I guess you can get bit or take in the infection through the passing of some human bodily fluid but not die right away.

Another difference is the water thing. In Max Brooks' work, the zombies are definitely dead so they cannot drown. They travel the globe skimming the murky bottom of the oceans and seas, coming ashore in far flung places like Iceland and the South Sea Islands. We're not so sure about our zom. The jury is still out as to just how dead they are, whether they keep any shred of their former humanity. I think about that female zom pushing the carriage filled with the rarest of sights - zombie toddlers. I still don't understand what it was I saw that day, but I know it was something both important and unique. And as for water, we see the zom through binoculars on the other side of the Hudson confused and startled by the river. When they drift across on boats it is because they fell or wandered on to the boats by accident.

I would say the biggest difference between the zombies created by Max Brooks and our real world zom are the maggots and worms and other bacteria. In *World War Z,* all parasites that normally invade and devour a rotting corpse sense the presence of the zombie virus and reject the potential host. Not true for what is going on here. Like I said earlier, we can already see the maggot infestations with our binoculars as we study the zom who make it to the other side of the barricade. It's pretty gross, the worms slithering in and out of their eye sockets and other openings. I guess the correct word is orifices. A lot of these guys are walking worm farms. No one ever packs a lunch for scout duty. Within minutes you'd just puke it up.

Will we ever get all the answers as to what has caused this pandemic, and when - if ever - it will stop? Or is this the new stage in human evolution? Is Earth destined now for zom and zom-kind only? I hear people posing these ideas around town and I begin to wonder if my friends and I are going to be the last of the human teenagers. Will we all wake up one day and decide together that we have had enough suffering and fling ourselves over the barricades screaming, "Come and get us, zom! You win!?" Crazy, man. Sometimes, these questions start to freak me out and I have to stop thinking. And writing. Now is one of those times. I'll write more later. I promise.

Friday, July 21, 2017

As I approach the two month anniversary of starting this diary (according to Mr. Chupka, the best English teacher ever, the "anni" part of anniversary refers to the Latin word for year, so I'm not sure if technically you can have a two month anniversary), I've begun to think of what it means for me to have this outlet. My primary motivation from the beginning has been to chronicle life in Hoboken during this time of the zom. But keeping this diary has also helped my head enormously. It has kept my brain from exploding everywhere, and given me one more friend at a time when friendship is like the most important possession.

We hear nothing from the outside world and have no idea whether there are people out there, like the military, trying to reach us with help. Planes stopped flying over head five months ago. The sky above belongs to just the birds again. It seems clear that the planet has come to a grinding halt. At some point a decision will have to be made whether to send an expedition out of Hoboken to search for other communities of survivors. We know of the one at Tudor City that Lily mentioned. The City Council has scheduled an open town meeting next week at Stevens Tech to discuss such an expedition. From what we know about zombies and water, we could easily sail a boat down the Hudson and up the East River to the United Nations. Tudor City sits on a bluff just above the U.N. Maybe there is some international body still meeting in a secret subterranean chamber of the U.N. trying to find a solution to the pandemic. Anything is possible. Until then, we sit and bake because I am sorry to report that the heat has returned, and this time with a vengeance.


Sunday, July 23, 2017

No moon tonight. I'm allowing myself five minutes of candle light to write. I was up on the roof with Tony Degrassi earlier this evening. He's maybe twenty years old and pretty cool and lives on the third floor with his parents. He owns a shortwave radio, but can only use it with special permission from the City Council since electricity is like gold and must be rationed and saved. If you owned a warehouse full of generators in Hoboken when this all began you'd be king now. Though you do need gasoline for those generators. That's something our bravest scavengers have to sneak out of Hoboken through the sewers to find.

Anyway, Tony and I were up on the roof looking at the constellations. Since there was no moon and no fluorescent light from the city, I could see stars and planets I'd never seen before. I spotted one constellation to the north that I thought looked like a girl, her head leaning to the left with hair to her shoulders. Tony said he had never noticed that one before and maybe I had discovered it, and under the laws of discovering constellations I should by right name it. He was probably just being nice. Tony definitely has what one would call paternal instincts. I hope he gets to become a father one day. He would be good at it.

I took Tony up on his offer of naming this new constellation and called it the Constellation Anne Frank. She deserved at least that. Tony thought it was a good name. I stared up at Anne and asked her to help me survive. I asked her to be my friend and warn me of anything bad coming so I could maybe stop it. I trust her. She will help me. I realize no one was there to help her, but from her diary I can tell she was the kind of girl of who believed in doing the right thing. If she were here now, a fourteen year old girl in Hoboken in 2017, she and I would be friends. I pray to Anne all the time like Grandma used to pray to Saint Theresa the Little Flower and Mary, the Blessed Mother. I suppose we all call on those we think will understand our predicament best.

## Wednesday, July 26, 2017

I borrowed Serena's copy of *The Definitive Edition of The Diary of a Young Girl: Anne Frank* and have been reading it again from cover to cover. Anne writes a lot about her friend Hanneli Goslar. It seems like Anne projects on to Hanneli all her fears regarding the slaughter of the Jews outside the secret annex, and worries constantly about her friend's fate. Anne also shares her feelings of guilt that even though conditions in hiding are far from ideal, she and her family are safe while Hanneli and her family are subject to the random brutality of the Nazis. Serena told me that ironically Anne died at Bergen-Belsen while Hanneli, also imprisoned there at the same time, managed to survive the war and eventually moved to Israel where she married and raised a family and had a full life.

Anne's thoughts on Hanneli got me to thinking about Ryan, who was with his family in Florida visiting his dying grandmother when the bottom fell out of our society and suddenly the zombie pandemic was touching every corner of the nation. If they had not traveled to Florida when they did, Ryan and his family would be here in Hoboken safe from the zom. But because of circumstance and unlucky choices, Ryan is out there somewhere with the zombie hordes, maybe trying to get back here, maybe a refugee in a similar community of survivors, or maybe a zombie himself now, moving with a pack of zom, looking for flesh, the dogs trailing along side him. I feel what Anne must have felt as she imagined Hanneli arrested by the Germans and sent to a concentration camp. Maybe in the end, history will repeat itself and Ryan will survive but I won't. So many stories are far from finished yet - mine, Ryan's, the zom's.

### Saturday, July 29, 2017

The town meeting took place yesterday in the large auditorium at Stevens Tech. The place was standing room only by the time the meeting got started. Various suggestions were offered by the crowd. Ultimately, the decision was made to send a boat containing 23 people, all who had military training at some point in their lives, down the Hudson and up the East River to the U.N. Complex. I thought

23 was a good omen since I began this diary on May 23rd, my birthday.

Then today happened, and parts of the mission may have to be rethought. I was at my bedroom window doing one of my scans of the Manhattan shore through Uncle Matt's telescope. I do this every day, just in case Dad and Uncle Matt are still alive and have made it to the water's edge. As I focused across the river, I heard a crowd below running toward the Hoboken waterfront from every direction. Someone yelled, "A ship! I see a ship!!" I turned my telescope toward where the crowd was pointing and saw the boat, one of the New York Waterway ferries. It was drifting across the river south and west with the current from midtown.

As I zoomed in closer I could make out figures on the deck, lots of them. And as the ferry continued drifting toward Hoboken I was able to see that this was not a group of escaping survivors, but a boatload of zom. They were walking into each other, arms flailing, blood everywhere on the deck. Several of them fell overboard while the ferry floated toward Hoboken as they mindlessly knocked into one another.

I screamed out, "No! It's not safe! Incoming zom!" When I realized the crowd could not hear me over their increasing calls that a boat of survivors was approaching, I ran barefoot down the eight flight of stairs to the side entrance of the building and out to the pier, shouting "No!" all the way. One of the river guards noticed me and called out, asking me what was wrong. I responded, "Zom!!!! The boat's full of zom!" He heard me and signaled the sharp shooters. Once the firing began, the crowd pushed back from the water and fled, now everyone screaming, "Zom!!!"

The boat nearly made it to Hoboken's shore. As the firing continued, one after another of the zom were taken out with a single shot to the head, either falling on the deck or tumbling over the rail into the water. The more the sharp shooters fired, the more zom poured on deck from below. There had to have been 300 or more of them. If that ferry had reached shore it could have proven disastrous. We make one mistake like allowing a ferry filled with zom to dock and Hoboken is finished.

I remained at the end of the pier and watched as each one was hit, trying to see if Dad or Uncle Matt was among them. Since the boat came from midtown I didn't think this was likely. But I stood and watched just in case. There seemed to be an equal distribution of male and female zom on the ferry, though some were so distorted from rotting that it was impossible to say who they might once have been. When the excursion sets sail for Tudor City and the U.N., I think some additional sharp shooters should be added to the group. There will be more boats like this one adrift in the waters around Manhattan. We can't allow ourselves to ever get caught off guard.

*Monday, July 31, 2017*

I'm up on my building's rooftop with Ginger checking the rain barrels after last night's much welcomed thunder and lightning storm. The booming began in the distance around dinner time. Then the sky opened up at nightfall and it rained as hard as I've ever seen. The coolest part was the lightning, strike after strike hitting the Empire State Building and the other skyscrapers, illuminating the city like the good old days. Too bad the zom aren't like turkeys, so stupid that they wander outside in a storm and put their heads back only to "drown" in the rain. If it rained bullets that might do the trick. Hopefully, some of those lightning strikes zapped a few zom smack in the head. That could easily have finished some of them off.

The barrels are full to their brims so it's time to spend the day filling jugs. I have to head downstairs and tell the super, Manny, who draws up a schedule whenever it rains with the building's tenants coming up in shifts until the barrels are empty and ready for the next storm. But I'm not rushing downstairs just yet. The sky is blue and clear with no chance of more rain. I can stay up here and write a little while longer.

Look at that city over there, once the capital of the world. It still looks magnificent, even now. Ginger is at my feet as I sit leaning against the useless air conditioning duct and write. The buildings remain standing in New York, but it's just a shell without the people. It's worse than bombed out Dresden after World War II. Endless destruction in the old black and white film footage they showed us in history class, but at least in Dresden people were left behind to rebuild. To the southeast at the end of Manhattan I can see the finally completed "Freedom Tower" of the new World Trade Center, constructed after so much fighting between adults about what should be on the site, but never completely occupied.

Dad told me that on 9/11 - the original 9/11 in 2001 before I was born - he stood on Stevens Hill just to my left and watched as the towers of the old World Trade Center exploded after the impact of the airplanes and then crashed to the ground. He was home from work that day, waiting for a furniture delivery. Mom was still working downtown at the time, just across the street from the Twin Towers at 7 World Trade Center, which caught fire and collapsed later in the day. The furniture being delivered was for a nursery. Not mine. Mom was pregnant in 2001, about six months into the pregnancy when 9/11 happened.

She evacuated her building with all her co-workers, but when the South Tower fell at 9:59 a.m. everyone in the streets panicked and ran. The crowd was desperate to get north, away from the debris and dust cloud that followed the collapse of the South Tower. Mom fell to the ground as everyone ran. She fell hard and couldn't get up. Her friends, Miriam and Elise, took her by the hands and walked with her as quickly as Mom could move until they found a paramedic near City Hall. Mom lost that baby when she fell in the stampeding crowd. It was a boy. My older brother. Killed on 9/11 before he even had a chance to be born. They named him Brendan, by the way. I sometimes think of Brendan. I wish he had lived so I would have a sixteen year old brother here with me today.

Uncle Matt told me recently that Mom came back from that loss after a couple of months, but Dad wasn't the same again until Mom found out she was pregnant with me in the early autumn of 2002. Once I was born, Dad found his way back to the living. It's sad what happens to people in this life. All those zom on that ferry the other day were men and women who had lives and loves and broken hearts just like Mom and Dad. But they lost the one thing that gets a person through the pain and sorrow. They lost their human consciousness, the thing that makes us live in hope after a loss, the thing that allows us to believe that joy will one day return. What I hope for them is that their souls have left their rotting bodies and made their way to an afterlife filled with happiness. I want Miranda to be wrong. I want the girl from my dream who I "killed" to be wrong. I don't want to think about a tiny shred of their old selves still lurking inside them now. It's bad enough that they turned into zombies. They shouldn't suffer as well.

## Wednesday, August 2, 2017

I don't know what to do, where to turn. I can't breathe today. I think about the reality of our situation. I think of the zom coming for us, constantly coming, wave after wave of them, a zombie tsunami. They will kill us. They will kill all of us - Mom and Ben and Lily and Mr. Rosen and Serena and Jason and Kahil and Miranda and Tony and Mary Rogers. They will just keep coming. We can't live here like this forever. We will lose. They will win.

Only Ginger would survive an all out zombie assault on the town. Poor Ginger, left behind alone to roam Jersey with the legions of other dogs traveling alongside the zom. If the end is imminent for all of us, I won't leave Ginger to suffer like that. For her, life without us would be suffering. I've promised her I'll make sure she leaves this world with us even if I have to kill her myself. I wonder if I have the strength and guts to strangle a dog.

## Thursday, August 3, 2017

I didn't mean what I wrote yesterday. That was crazy. I don't give up. I won't give up. They will not kill all of us. This doesn't end here, now, like this in Hoboken, New Jersey. We will outlive the zom. I will grow up to be a man and live a full life. I am not dying at fourteen. And I am not letting Ben die at eight.

*Monday, August 7, 2017*

An exciting day on the barricade. I was on scout duty with Miranda and Serena, just me and the girls. Jason said last week that Serena likes me as more than a friend. I think she likes me only as a friend, though by saying "only" I don't mean to diminish being someone's friend. I think Jason actually likes Serena, even though he usually goes for blonds and I can't recall him ever before having a crush on an African American girl. Sometimes on scout duty I watch Jason watching Serena and I see how he looks at her. I think he brought up the whole idea of Serena liking me to see what I would say. I told him the truth, like I said, that I think she thinks of me as a friend and that is the way I think of her. He seemed relieved when I responded the way I did, making me believe even more that Jason likes Serena as more than a friend.

But does that stuff even matter now? As I started to write before I went off topic again, this afternoon Serena was scanning south with her binoculars while Miranda and I were watching west. In the distance, coming from the highway that leads east to the Holland Tunnel and west to the drawbridges, a vehicle appeared. I hadn't seen a moving car or truck for several months. This was an SUV with a missing windshield, and whoever was driving had their foot pressed hard on the gas pedal, almost flipping the vehicle over as they made sharp turns around piles of debris and abandoned cars. Behind the SUV about a tenth of a mile were the zom, hundreds of them running as fast as I've ever seen them run in the daylight and heat. Serena sounded the alarm - all zombie scouts were recently given air horns for guard duty after several cases were discovered in the basement of a building on Willow Street.

As I watched the vehicle approach, I said to Serena and Miranda, "This guy is going to crash the barricade," which is something that we just could not let happen since the zom would pour through the opening. So I steadied myself, gun in hand, and waited to see what the driver would do. I would never shoot a living human being, but I would certainly shoot out a car's tire to keep it from smashing the barricade. I was about to shoot the left front tire when the SUV came to a screeching halt. Two adults and four kids jumped out and ran toward the barricade screaming to be let into Hoboken. I turned my gun on the zom and began to take them out one by one as they neared the panicked family. Shots rang out from all along the barricade as a crew below quickly cleared a small opening so the survivors could enter.

The Conners from West Orange were lucky. Lots of people have probably attempted the trip and not made it, given what Mr. Conner told us about Route 280. West Orange to Hoboken was not a long trip, maybe a half hour in the before days. But it took the Conners ten times that long to get here given that they couldn't travel on 280 since it was crawling with zom wandering up and down the highway. Mr. Connor said that as they approached the Holland Tunnel, they encountered the pack of zombies that chased them to the barricade, hundreds of them stumbling out of the tunnel's mouth, climbing over abandoned cars left everywhere during those crazy last days when Hoboken sealed itself off from the world and New Yorkers tried to flee the onslaught.

There is a full moon again tonight. I can keep writing until all hours so long as I position myself just right at the window in my bedroom. The refugees making it to Hoboken lately are fewer and far between. And with each new arrival we hear tales of an increasingly hostile zom-ruled world. Darkness is descending everywhere on the planet and I long for the days of my childhood when the future wasn't this reality. I miss spending my time at the skateboard park with Ryan, going to school, watching television. But when I write these things down - the simplicity of my childhood - it all seems so superficial and unimportant. Strangely, I feel more alive than I did during those before days. What I do now when I get up each morning has a significance to it. Every day is pure adrenaline.

At moments like this, however, when it's late and quiet (except for the intermittent howl echoing from across the river) the reality of life hits me like a pail of ice water. I don't feel more alive. I feel trapped and frightened. At night my existence strikes me as borrowed time. I think this is how Mom must feel most days. I understand why she can't get out of bed some mornings. All of us here in Hoboken - like all people everywhere in the world that have survived to this point - have a terminal illness that is trying everyday to penetrate the barricades and finish us off. Mom isn't able to distract herself from these thoughts as easily as I am. Poor Mom. Everything would be different for her if only Dad was here with us.

## Saturday, August 12, 2017

We're approaching the anniversary of my grandmother's death in 2010. I was seven years old and it really is the first summer I can remember in vivid detail, how sick she became that July and how quickly she declined, ultimately ending up in hospice care, comatose on morphine. All those trips with Mom and Dad and Uncle Matt to the hospital. Ben was only a baby and has no recollection of the events of that summer. But I remember all of it. Grandma was Dad and Uncle Matt's mother. She was kind and gentle and very old, almost 86. Her death was my first loss, and standing by her bedside with Dad was how I learned about dying. We had a wake for her and a Funeral Mass. Flowers and photographs from throughout her life filled the viewing room at the funeral parlor in Livingston. It was a life celebrated as well as mourned. It was how we used to do things. People died and we grieved their leaving us, but we returned at a certain point to the world of the living. It's not how we do things now.

There have been deaths in Hoboken from old-time "natural" causes since January. Cancer, heart attacks, the occasional accident, all still happen. They are mourned but not the same way as before. Births occur as well, though they're not as common as deaths. We're eight months into this. I doubt nine months from now, if there are people left in Hoboken, that we'll see any births. I'm sure people will continue to get pregnant. That's not the same thing as having a baby, though. Serena says women are choosing to terminate pregnancies early rather than have babies who are purposely born into a world of zombies. I can understand that decision. But if we figure out how to destroy the zom and win, we're going to have to have a lot of babies fast to repopulate the world.

Hoboken has no grave yards so the only choice is to bury folks at sea, dropped off the edge of Pier A to float out to the Atlantic Ocean. I remember that Ben and I used to go with Dad and Uncle Matt to visit Grandma's grave at Gate of Heaven Cemetery in East Hanover. All those rows of tombstones dating back to the 1940s. I remember endless tombstones as tall as me, a sea of them, when Grandma was buried there on a sunny August day in 2010. The idea of burying your dead and having a grave to visit seems so weird to me now. But Grandma got a visit on every major holiday, and every now and then on an ordinary autumn or spring Saturday just because it was a beautiful day and Dad or Uncle Matt thought new flowers should be planted.

I miss Grandma, how she smelled, how her house smelled. She had the most frail, bony hands. I miss how she covered us with kisses when we walked through her front door. I even miss how she couldn't hear well and you had to repeat everything twice to her. It seems like another lifetime on a different planet when we used to visit her grave at the cemetery, let alone at her house when she was still alive. I'm glad Grandma left Earth before the zombie pandemic. I think of her stuck alone at her house when the outbreak began and imagine how afraid she would have been. She would never have made it. I bet as many elderly people as children have been devoured by the zom. The smallest and weakest have never been able to put up much of a fight at any time in human history. Why should this apocalypse have been any different?

## Tuesday, August 22, 2017

I haven't written for over a week. There are days when I feel like Mom, so depressed I can't even think of opening this diary. Usually, it lasts just a day. But for the entire past week I was only partly present for the events of my life. When you stare into the Black Hole and see how dark and never-ending it is, the ability to go on becomes a real struggle.

I think about Anne crammed into that attic for over two years with seven other people, falling also into the depths of despair. In some entries you can hear the sadness and fear between her words. She tries hard to not give in to the despair, but it must have been difficult for the eight of them to go on from day to day. More so, maybe, than I can comprehend. This has all happened before to people, or at least a version of it. It is happening now. And if we survive the zom as a species, humankind will find themselves back here again one day. Trapped. Hunted. Waiting to be exterminated. This isn't an easy world to navigate.

## Thursday, August 24, 2017

The expedition boat to the U.N. and Tudor City sailed this morning at 8:00 a.m. Thousands of people lined the waterfront. Mr. Rosen said it reminded him of the crowd on the dock in Hamburg when he left Europe for America in 1947 after spending two years in a displaced persons camp in Germany. Lately, I'm noticing that Mr. Rosen slips more and more between the present and the past. Some days you can look at him sitting in the corner of the apartment staring out the window and you know that his mind is somewhere in Poland, either before or during the war. What he has to remember is so terrible - the ghettos, the cattle cars, Treblinka, his murdered family, Yaacov dying in his arms. I hope I'm wrong and on those days when he seems so distant he is with his wife at their cabin in the Catskills in a town called Phoenicia, where I know Mr. Rosen was at his most happy ever.

The heat is brutal today. Even at 8:00 a.m. the sweat poured down my face and neck. The crowd made it all the hotter. But I must admit there was a feeling of hope, even joy in the air, along with our collective funk. This venture might result in direct contact with another community of survivors. And maybe they've already made contact with yet another group somewhere else. The rebuilding of modern society might begin with this voyage. What was it that Anne heard Winston Churchill say on the radio? "Now this is not the end. It is not even the beginning of the end. But it is, perhaps, the end of the beginning." We sure could use a Winston Churchill now.

## Friday, August 25, 2017

According to the lookouts stationed at the farthest southeast corner of the waterfront, our ship made it into New York Harbor past the Statue of Liberty yesterday. Then it passed out of sight as it turned up the East River. They have been gone one night now and some people are starting to whisper that the worst has happened. I think this is ridiculous speculation, because even if contact was made immediately with Tudor City there would have to be a meeting and some exchange of information. There is no way they could have gotten there and back in such a short period of time. I have faith that this voyage will be a success. Even though it is doubtful since they were both downtown that last day, Dad and Uncle Matt could be in Tudor City. It is possible. If they could come back to us I know my mother would return to her old self the moment she heard my father say her name, "Kate." I can hear his voice saying it now. I miss his voice.

## Saturday, August 26, 2017

They still haven't returned. We sit here and wait. Lining the waterfront, hanging out apartment windows, people remain quiet as they stare south toward the harbor. Tony has been authorized to use his shortwave radio for a full hour in the morning and an hour in the evening in case there is a broadcast transmission from the expedition, who understood these would be the times of day we'd be on the radio waiting to hear from them.

Hoboken was an oven today as the temperature reached 100 degrees. We've never had this experience before, someone leaving and we wait for their return. No one has ventured across the river or to the other side of the barricades since the television went out, other than a quick, short trip for supplies. But it had to be done. Even with growing vegetables and fruit on rooftops and in the parks, catching fish from the Hudson, and severely rationing the stockpile of canned goods collected and distributed by the City Council, we will eventually run out of food. And when we do it will be an even more horrendous existence for the 250,000+ people crammed into this one square mile. There have to be other survivors and we need to connect with them so we can make progress and rebuild the world. I've become so thin, as have Ben and Mom and Lily and Mr. Rosen. Poor, sweet Ginger was skin and bones when she arrived here, and that hasn't changed. If the zom do manage to penetrate the barricades, they will surely be disappointed to find no meat on any of us.

## Sunday, August 27, 2017

No ship. No news. No shortwave radio transmissions. If we never hear from them again it will be a blow to this community that I am not certain people can survive. As we sit and wait, though, life in Hoboken must go on. I am scheduled for scout duty this afternoon. The zom must be kept at bay. It's sweltering in that tower. We're up there practically just in our underwear. There is no other way to make it through a daytime shift. The good news is that the zom who wander along the other side of the barricade appear to be affected by the extreme heat as much as us. We've noticed that in them before. The bad news is that they are rotting at a wickedly fast rate, some of them practically nothing more than skeletons with chomping jaws and just a few bits of decomposing flesh hanging from their frames. I say that's bad news because the odor is nothing I can adequately describe here. I thought we were all used to it, but this new stench is worse than vomit and shit. A world filled with corpses out walking in the August sun is a world where the stench of death has replaced all other smells.

We don't experience the sweet fragrance of flowers or the whiff of springtime rain. No more of that wonderful smell a baby has, lotion and talcum powder mixed with new life. Mom's chocolate chip cookies will never come out of the oven again and reach my room with their aroma. There is no more enjoying the wonderful smells of dinner cooking on the stove or the beautiful scent of pine when the Christmas tree (if we ever even have Christmas trees again) is dragged home and set up in the corner of the living room. No more smell of burning leaves in the fall or salt water at the beach in the summer. And my favorite smell, fresh buttered popcorn at the movies, gone forever. Even odors I wasn't wild about are gone, like hot tar fumes when they paved the road and wet dog fur in the building elevator on a rainy day. The zom have invaded our noses and completely taken over. They remind us with every breath that this is their world now and we are banished to this one little corner of it.

## Monday, August 28, 2017

At approximately 1:30 p.m. today a ship was spotted floating in New York Harbor. It looked like the one that left us with 23 aboard last Thursday, but according to the river lookouts there was no sign of life on the boat as it drifted with the current around the harbor. No one knows what this means. Is it even the same boat? Are the 23 who sailed out of Hoboken still alive? It's unlikely the boat was overrun by zom if there is no sign of movement on the deck. We would definitely see signs of zombie activity if that had been their fate. The deck would at least be covered in blood. Could they be trapped somewhere on the East Side of Manhattan, separated from their only means of escape? The City Council will hold an emergency meeting to decide what we do next.

Lily just arrived back at the apartment after waiting outside City Hall with hundreds of others while the City Council met. The decision was made to send a small investigative boat out to the harbor. Four police officers have volunteered to make the trip. In the meantime, unless it's my imagination, there seems to be an increase in guttural moaning echoing off the buildings across the river. The zom sound on the war path. Not that it's possible for them to act with any purpose or intent. At least, so we think.

Mom is opening a can of beans to be shared by the five of us (six if you count Ginger, who always gets some of everyone's share, even Mom's). Mr. Rosen is doing his best to add taste and stretch the meal with a few of his herbs. The sun has finally begun to set but the apartment remains an oven. It must be unbearable in apartments on the other side of town away from the waterfront, especially if there is no cross ventilation. Every few minutes, Ben runs back to our bedroom window, which gives the best view of the river looking south, especially through Uncle Matt's telescope.

The boat that may or may not be ours has floated toward Ellis Island. Grandma's mother, my great-grandmother, passed through Ellis Island in 1911 when she emigrated alone at seventeen from Ireland. I think Mom's father's family arrived there from Scotland around the same time. Has it been overridden by zom now? Zombies dragging themselves around the Great Hall where immigrants once waited for processing to enter America. Or is Ellis Island empty and available as a possible outpost for Hoboken? We have to start thinking about rebuilding the New York metropolitan area. We need to find isolated, safe spots along both rivers in order to set up additional communities and slowly the world will become ours once more. It's the 17th century all over again and Manhattan Island and the Hudson River, along with the rest of the New World, have to be explored and conquered anew. I'm sure that was Native American-phobic. But are there even any Native Americans left to insult? Dinner is ready. I'll write with the latest news tomorrow.

## Tuesday, August 29, 2017

The boat was ours and it was empty. No sign of life or zom. No one knows what that means and I'm trying not to think about it. Activity increased along the barricade today so we had plenty to distract us. This morning, as she scouted the western horizon, Miranda yelled, "Incoming!" Easily a thousand of them came clawing and stumbling over each other with the dogs in close pursuit. At the same time, a hundred or so poured out of the entrance to the PATH train, where normally there is only a small trickle of one or two at a time.

The sharp shooters got quite a workout, doing their best to hit the zom and not the dogs, and then it was time for the ZDC to remove the corpses and dump them in the lime pit. With the heat what it is today, again over 100 degrees, the work of the ZDC couldn't wait until morning when zom activity is at a minimum. So Miranda, Jason and I watched the distance for more incoming. A few zom continued to show up in groups of four and five. They had to be taken out before they approached any further so the ZDC could complete its enormous task without incident. I wonder why they arrive in waves. Sometimes fifty. Other times a hundred or more. Today a thousand. They must travel like that, attracting stray ones as they migrate. New Jersey must be nothing now but a zombie wasteland.

## Sunday, September 3, 2017

Labor Day Weekend, so different than last year's when Dad and Mom and Ben and I drove up to Cape Cod. We stayed in a cedar shingle cottage in Dennis Port with white shutters and window boxes filled with bright red geraniums. We swam in the warm water of Nantucket Sound and ate lobster and played miniature golf and never imagined where we'd find ourselves a year later. A deep depression has settled over the town. Since the police scouting party towed our empty boat back to Pier A, the residents of Hoboken have felt more trapped and hopeless than ever. We had so much optimism when the boat set off. That optimism is completely gone.

Lily feels guilty since she was the one who told us about Tudor City when she arrived. Mom told her that whatever has happened is not her fault, and added that we should hold on to hope since the 23 who left on the boat all have military training and will find a way to return to us. I admire Mom, her ability to speak hopefully despite her depression. I think she is stronger than I sometimes give her credit. But even in the best of times a child's relationship with his or her mother is often not easy. In a time of stress it only gets worse. Anne wrote in her diary about life in hiding with a mother she didn't understand, who didn't understand her either. Don't get me wrong. I love my mother. I just wish that I could return to the days of my childhood and not feel the weight of so much responsibility, back when I was the kid and she was the mom.

## Wednesday, September 6, 2017

Another month and another full moon. Today's edition of the Hoboken Reporter was dedicated solely to news and speculation about the missing 23 explorers. The favorite pastime of town residents has become standing along the waterfront with binoculars scanning the river and harbor as well as the shore of Manhattan for any sign of life. The pendulum swings for most of us between utter despair that the 23 have been killed and complete belief that they will appear one day sailing around the tip of Manhattan in a new boat with "United Nations" printed on the side.

September has not brought much relief from the heat and humidity, with the thermometer topping 90 degrees most days. Mr. Rosen has expanded his window sill herb garden and we look forward to when we will have fresh radishes, spinach, carrots, and tomatoes. Ben has started fishing every day with a group of young boys at the end of Pier A. Fluke, flounder, striped bass, and blue fish have all been plentiful. I know we must continue to find new food sources to feed a quarter million people, but I never thought pigeon would become a big part of our diet. It has and it actually doesn't taste that bad when properly cooked, though that's another challenge. Most people prepare their dinner at communal open fire pits. We have one on the large public terrace off the fourth floor of our building. It must be carefully supervised or else the entire building could go up in flames.

Firewood is also at a premium, and the search for alternative fuel sources will soon become a priority for Hoboken.

I can hear Mom and Lily talking in the kitchen. They are sharing a bottle of wine. In the pantry, Dad stocked away what I'm told is an excellent wine collection. Every so often Mom and Lily open a bottle. It usually coincides with the full moon when I'm up late writing, so I catch bits and pieces of their conversation. Mom misses Dad and Lily misses Doug. They share memories. Tonight Mom is telling Lily about when Dad asked her to marry him on a bitter cold night during a snowstorm in front of the Rockefeller Center Christmas Tree. No one was around except some tourists from Denmark, who applauded after Dad got down on one knee and gave Mom a ring. Then Mom and Dad and the Danes went to an Irish pub for Guinness stout and shepherd's pie (whatever that is) to celebrate. That was 1999 - another century. It may as well have been the 18th or 19th century, seeing how foreign it is to our lives now.

Lily told Mom about her early days with Doug in Williamsburg, Brooklyn. Both of them were young hipsters hoping for their break when Doug found an agent for his novel about a fictional chance meeting in 1917 Paris between the poet e.e. cummings (that's how he signed all his poems, with lower case letters) and the writer and art patron Gertrude Stein (never heard of her until now). You learn a lot staying up late at night listening to adults discuss life over a bottle of wine. Once the book was sold to a publisher, they moved to Jane Street in the West Village. All was wonderful beyond Lily's expectation of how wonderful life could be. Then Passenger Zero arriving from Rio went berserk at Kennedy Airport and twenty-four hours later the local news and all the cable news stations began reporting on riots in Canarsie and Howard Beach. But they weren't riots at all. They were swift and sudden catastrophic zombie outbreaks.

Lily says it happened so fast in Manhattan that most people had little time to react. She remembers that day - the day of Dad's last trip into the city - when it crossed the line in Manhattan from pockets of outbreak to extinction level event. People were out on the streets everywhere rushing to banks and stores, and trying to reach train and bus stations to leave the city. Like footage of the 2004 Indian Ocean Tsunami, the 2011 Pacific Tsunami in Japan, and the 2016 Atlantic/Caribbean Tsunami, a wave of zom poured over the bridges from Brooklyn and out of every subway station. They began attacking and biting people. Usually not devouring most of the adults, but leaving them to "die" and join the howling horde. Most people died within minutes of being bit, if not seconds.

One of Lily's strangest memories from that day were the cell phones. As thousands of zom flooded the streets of Manhattan, phones could be heard ringing in all their pockets. Crazy, man. The people in their lives were trying to reach these zom, unaware they had already crossed over. My guess would be many calls went unanswered that day.

As Lily ran with the panicked mob away from the crazed zom, the ringing of cell phones was almost loud enough to drown out the screams of the living and the moaning of the dead. I bet that day is when we lost Dad and Uncle Matt.

Oh God, I wish Dad was here for Mom, and Doug was here for Lily. And I wish Uncle Matt was here with Tolstoy, as well as his new boyfriend Jed. I only met Jed a few times but he seemed to really love Uncle Matt, and I was happy - maybe relieved, too - that I wouldn't have to worry any longer about Uncle Matt growing old alone with his cat. But all these men - Dad, Doug, Uncle Matt, Jed - have probably been swallowed up already by the zombie tsunami. I am the man left here in this home to do what has to be done to keep us alive. Dad, where are you? Should I be looking up to the sky and heaven when I talk to you, or across the river at that desolate city?

*Saturday, September 9, 2017*

I stared at Miranda tonight in the waning moonlight (Lily taught me the difference between a waxing moon and a waning moon the other day). We were sharing scout duty with a new guy named Peter, one of the Conner kids who escaped from West Orange with his brothers and sister and parents back in early August. Peter is a good guy and a quick study as a zombie scout, though he doesn't say much when he's up in that tower watching the horizon through his binoculars. I think Peter saw a lot when he was out in the zom wilderness that the rest of us kids couldn't even imagine, and he keeps all of that buried deep inside himself.

Miranda scanned the opposite direction from Peter. The moonlight hit her long brown hair at just the right angle so that it appeared to shimmer. Her intense focus on the southern horizon was mesmerizing. She is a strange girl but she is such a good and kind and well-meaning person. Her face is beautiful in that way an offbeat face with lots of character turns out to be beautiful once you see the person behind it. I want to add only that Miranda has perfect ears. Her long brown hair was pushed behind both ears and all night I wanted to kiss one of those ears, feel my mouth against her skin for just a moment.

It was probably a good thing that Peter was up there with us or I might have done something stupid like told her I loved her, or something else equally lame. From what Lily was saying the other night, I should have recited an e.e. cummings poem to her, ". . . . your slightest look easily will unclose me. . . ." That's all I remember from e.e. cummings.

Better yet, I could have tried that old John Denver song Dad used to sing - badly - when he wanted to serenade Mom, "You fill up my senses. Like a night in the forest. . . ." It's so corny, but I love that song. It reminds me of Dad. I find myself singing it in my head sometimes without even thinking about it. I'll be going about my business and there it just is suddenly in my head.

Good night, Miranda. Sweet dreams, if sweet dreams are still possible. I will do my best to get you a world in which we can grow old, a world where we can be together without fear of zom. Miranda will travel with me and Ben to the moon. We will become space pioneers and play a part in saving the human race.

## Monday, September 11, 2017

I thought Mom would want to stay in bed today and hide from the world. I was wrong. To her credit, she got up early and made us fried potatoes over the fourth floor fire pit. Lily commented over breakfast that it was such a beautiful, sunny, clear day. Mom said that was what always annoyed her most about the original 9/11, how everyone kept saying that it had been such a beautiful day and acted like that was the thing that surprised them most about the day. Not that two hijacked commercial jetliners crashed into the towers of the World Trade Center and killed 3,000 people. And another crashed into the Pentagon. And a fourth into a field in Pennsylvania when the passengers fought back. Just that it had happened on such a beautiful, sunny, clear day.

At 8:46 a.m., the moment the first airplane hit the North Tower, a procession began from City Hall to the memorial on Pier A for the 39 residents of Hoboken who died on 9/11. Hoboken had the most casualties of any New Jersey town that day. People looking both weary and defiant marched carrying American flags and a few had scraggly flowers, mostly weeds they picked along the way. I walked with Mom and Ben for Brendan. That was our silent purpose for being there. Mr. Rosen insisted on accompanying us. Lily held his arm the entire time.

When we reached the memorial, the crowd spontaneously sang the national anthem. Everyone seemed to get a little choked up. I saw grown men shedding tears. As far as we know here in the Democratic People's Republic of Hoboken, we are America. We could be all there is left. The last stand could take place on our soil. We better start acting like it. "La Resistance lives on!", as they sing in the supremely brilliant and funny *South Park* movie, which I would give anything to watch right now for both inspiration and a much needed laugh.


Wednesday, September 13, 2017

This morning an old woman, African American with hardly any hair on her head in a pink housecoat and bedroom slippers, appeared suddenly wandering around the debris on the other side of the barricade. Miranda spotted her first and said, "I can't tell if she's zom or not," so she squinted more intently through her binoculars. The old woman then got close enough to the barricade so that we could all see she was fully human. I climbed down the tower with Peter and we both began moving sandbags, creating as small an opening as possible for one of us to crawl out. Peter is a pretty big kid, so naturally I went through the hole to the other side.

"Hurry, Jack," Miranda yelled down to me as she scanned the horizon. I got to my feet and ran a direct line to the woman. I startled her when I took hold of her thin arm and escorted her back, forcing her down and under the barricade.

"Jack, quick! Incoming zom!!" Miranda screamed.

I looked up and saw one barreling toward me. Peter pulled the woman through the hole. Then I made it under, just as the zom grabbed hold of my shoe. My heart stopped. I was so frightened I lost my ability to scream, or make any sound except a panicky whimper. I kicked my legs as hard as I could and got free, sliding safely through minus my shoe. I could hear more zom amassing on the other side. The first zom, a male with brown hair dripping blood and skin off his face, appeared growling in the hole. One shot rang out. Straight into his forehead. He slumped over, his body blocking the other zom from penetrating the barricade. I turned to my left and saw Miranda standing there holding the gun I'd left up in the tower. She was shaking and didn't move until I called out her name.

When she ran to me she was still shaking. We examined my leg. No bites. Thank God. I had never been touched by a zom before, not even the girl I "killed". This could have been it for me. The sharp shooters arrived, positioning themselves along the top of the barricade, and began to systematically take out the remaining zom.

While Miranda helped me stand, Peter tended to the woman. She was in a total daze, not able to tell us anything about how she got there. A crowd began to form. With all the zom now dead or retreating (well, wandering away), a group of men started to repair the barricade. One of them told everyone to stand back as he swung an ax and chopped the male zombie with brown hair in two, the one who grabbed my leg. I didn't think there was anything left that could make me sick, but I choked back puke when he had to swing a second and then a third time to finish the job. Another man pushed the lower extremities of the zom corpse to the other side with a two-by-four, then shoved the upper half through. The hole was filled tight with a quadruple layer of sandbags, the severed corpse left for the ZDC to drag to the lime pit later.

I questioned my decision at first to help the woman since it endangered the entire town, but everyone has said they would have done the same thing. We acted swiftly and got her to safety. How could we sit helplessly in that tower and watch her devoured by a swarm of zom? As it turned out, pinned to the inside of her pocket she had an envelope with a letter written by her daughter explaining that her mother was named Sadie Turner. She was 81 and from Newark, and she had dementia. We'll never know how Sadie made it to Hoboken. Had she been with someone until almost the end? Her daughter, perhaps, who scrawled the letter at some point when she realized her mother might find herself alone in the zom wilderness? You don't have to worry about her any more, Cassie Morton (that was the daughter's name). Your mother is safe here with us. We will take care of her. I'm sure that tonight I'll have nightmares about my close encounter with a zombie, but I'm happy we saved her. Sadie Turner is one more survivor among a quarter million people, and that counts enormously in this world.

I'm trying to go to sleep and I find myself thinking of Miranda, how she must feel this night after her first "kill". I wish I was with her, holding her in my arms, telling her everything will be OK. She shot that zom to save my life. I will always be grateful to her for that, especially since I know it was not an easy thing for her to do. If she had not been there and taken the brave and swift action she did, I would have been mauled. Whatever the outcome of that, I certainly wouldn't be here now writing these words. Miranda saved my life.

*Sunday, September 17, 2017*

Miranda has been understandably distant since Wednesday. I will give her some time and space. I know from personal experience that she needs to think through what happened in her own way. The first time you do it - shoot one of them in the head or pound their brains with a crowbar - it feels like you killed an actual person. In time, taking out zom gets much easier for all of us. I guess that's actually a good thing, that it gets easier, since we have no choice.

There was an announcement in the last Hoboken Reporter that officials want to reopen schools. For now only grammar school through the seventh grade will be mandatory; older kids are needed to fill their roles in running the town. That means I can continue manning the Observer barricade. It will be good for Ben to be back in a structured classroom again. Of course, without electricity and so much else you need to run a school, this will be a challenge for the town. But I believe it is another sign of hope when a community decides to invest resources in the education of its kids. It is saying to ourselves and the world - we will survive as a society 10, 20, 30 years from now and our children need to be educated in order to become productive leaders of that future society.

Mom woke up this morning and announced that she wanted to go to church. I'm jumping around here, I know. Anyway, we haven't been to Mass in ages. I'm not really speaking to God at the moment. Frankly, I'm pissed at him. Don't know how else to put it. And sitting in a church begging the creator of everything, including the zom, to save us seems pointless to me. Nevertheless, Ben and I got dressed and walked with Mom to Our Lady of Grace over on Church Square Park. Father Murphy said the Mass. I was surprised at how many people filled the church. As I sat there in the packed pew, I realized that I actually missed going to church - the singing, the stained glass, the smell of incense, the feeling of being close to God. I didn't feel all that anger toward him once I was there. I just felt worn out.

Father Murphy prayed for the missing 23 explorers, that God returns them to us safe and sound. He prayed for all our missing friends and family. He prayed for the planet, that humankind would somehow find a cure for the zombie pandemic. He also prayed for the zom themselves, that their souls find rest in heaven with God. This last part moved me more than I could have expected. I found myself thinking of Miranda.

As I looked around the church at the faces, I noticed that everyone, no matter their age or race or gender, seemed deep in thought talking to God, begging him to save Hoboken and save the world. Mom stared up at the altar as she mumbled all the prayers to herself, this intense expression on her face. My mother's beautiful, sad face, so thin and aged in less than a year. I don't know if I will continue to attend Mass every Sunday, but I will go back if it helps Mom. It's not easy being a single mother in a city under siege during a zombie apocalypse. If she finds peace in going to church, who am I to judge her? Who am I to judge anything at this point?

## Thursday, September 21, 2017

We have figured out how to deal with one of Hoboken's biggest problems - rodents. The rat population has increased along with the human population, only at a scary huge rate. They chase each other on the sidewalks and in the gutters, rushing in and out of every sewer grate with no fear. Small children are bit every day as they play along side the rats, fighting for space in the same alleys and gutters. But food shortage concerns have given rise to a new delicacy that I suppose was unavoidable - roasted rat on a stick. Vendors with push carts sell them up and down Washington Street. Most of us lost our gag reflex long ago, and for a citizenry in desperate need of new food sources, especially protein, rat meat has surprising taste and nutritional value.

Miranda has started to bounce back from our close call with the zom. She doesn't want to talk about it, but says she has come to understand what had to be done. We're noticing more and more that there are large packs of zom swarming no man's land. Lately, they seem more restless, and fling themselves against the barricade, often getting stabbed by the barbed wire that's been added to reinforce the sandbags and bricks and mangled debris that make up our only protection against them. Once stuck, they continue writhing and howling until a bullet through the head shuts them up forever. A problem with the increased zom activity is that we are running through more ammunition, which will eventually run out. Whenever possible, a swift blow to the skull with an ax or shovel or crowbar must be used instead.

Most days are still hot, but at night you can feel a hint of autumn in the air, which makes sleeping much easier. There is nothing more wonderful now to me than a cool breeze, even if it carries the stench of zom with it. It's amazing what you can get up and face in the morning if you've slept for eight or nine hours. School is scheduled to reopen on Monday, October 2$^{nd}$, and Ben is already grumbling that it's unfair he has to go and I don't. I tell him that he's the lucky one. I would love to study history and geography and literature and science again. Even math.

The new school curriculum was published in the paper and it does include these subjects. But reflecting the times in which we live, it also includes first aid, municipal security, finding alternative water sources, and zombie pathology and behavior. At any point, one of us could happen upon a chance encounter with a zom - even a five or six year old child - and it is really important that everyone in Hoboken know how to deal with this possible situation. You don't crawl in a ball and play dead on the ground like when meeting a bear in the wild. The zom won't just sniff at you and wander away. They will tear you apart without a moment's hesitation. Rip out your insides, devouring every organ if they can, leaving you just a pile of bones for the dogs to sniff at, chew, and maybe bury. The only way to deal with a zombie confrontation is either run to a place of safety or stay and smash in its skull. There aren't really any other options.

## Tuesday, September 26, 2017

The 23 sailed from Hoboken over a month ago. I doubt they will ever return. I think human life has been extinguished in New York City. I can't imagine there are many like Lily left who survive on their own wits and stay one step ahead of the zom. Autumn has arrived here in Hoboken, which means winter is not far behind. Will a quarter million people be able to survive winter, particularly if it is a bad one? It will be interesting to see how the zom react to frigid cold and perhaps even snow. Last winter was so mild, as were the three winters before that. We haven't had a real winter since I was a little kid.

I remember the Christmas blizzard of 2010 and the almost weekly snow and ice storms that followed throughout the winter of 2011. Then there was the cold and snow of 2013 following Hurricane Sandy. When I tell Ben about two feet of snow piled in the streets he looks at me like I'm crazy. He has no memory of making a snowman (sorry, Serena and Miranda, I should say "snow person") with Dad on the soccer field across Frank Sinatra Drive from our building. But there was such a winter in my lifetime as well as his. I remember making that snowman with Dad, and snow angels, too. I remember the two feet of snow. I remember so much, but where are those memories going to end up? Didn't all the zom once have life experiences that made up their past? All those memories, all that life, disappeared for each of them with a single bite from someone who had already crossed over. It seems our past is as tenuous (good word; learned it from Lily) as our present and future.

Friday, September 29, 2017

I went home with Miranda today after we finished morning scout duty, which had been an uneventful four hours, my favorite kind of zombie scout shift. The only activity on the other side was a seriously decomposed male zom who wandered by the barricade around 10:00 a.m., unable to walk after his foot got stuck between two cement blocks. We never shoot solo zom if they're not trying to penetrate the barricade since it wouldn't accomplish anything other than call more zom. This one, still wearing the remains of a suit and tie, shuffled by with two dogs at his tail scarfing down scraps as they fell from his face and neck. Miranda, Jason and I were watching him to see what he would do once his foot got stuck. He tugged at it a few times, appearing genuinely confused when it wouldn't move, then stumbled forward as his right leg tore off at the ankle. The three of us let out a collective, "Gross!" But he didn't miss a beat and kept walking, well, limping away from the barricade with the dogs in tow. I watched him slowly, very slowly, disappear into the distance, dragging his right leg as he figured out how to move with his weight mostly on his left foot, the one still attached to his body.

As we walked home, Miranda and I joked about how disgusting it was, amazed once again that there was something new that could make us nauseous. When we reached her brownstone on Hudson Street she asked me if I'd like to come in for lunch. I said yes so long as she wasn't serving chicken legs, which made her laugh. I knew then that she liked me since what I said was so stupid and didn't even make sense. If there had been something clever to say about serving a foot, then maybe I would have deserved the laugh.

There were a dozen scrawny little kids playing on Miranda's stoop as we entered the building. Inside, three railroad apartments and a basement studio house nine families, one being Miranda and her mother. Before the zombie pandemic, Miranda lived across the river in a loft in Tribeca in downtown Manhattan. Mrs. Jelinek, her mother, was a fashion designer who had the smarts to pack two suitcases, grab Miranda, and hop on the PATH train to Hoboken after Passenger Zero arrived at Kennedy from Rio.

"Mom," Miranda called out as we entered their room and a half on the second floor with a shared bath. "Jack came home with me."

Mrs. Jelinek emerged through the curtains that separated her room from Miranda's sleeping nook. She smiled at me and asked how my family was holding up, standard stuff. At first I couldn't figure out why she seemed so uneasy with me. Then, when Miranda raised the issue of lunch Mrs. Jelinek explained that she only had two eggs but would find a way to make do for the three of us. I felt terrible once I understood why she was so uncomfortable. She was ashamed that she didn't have more to offer me. As much as I wanted to stay and spend time with Miranda away from the lookout tower, I couldn't bring myself to eat either of those eggs. I thanked Miranda and Mrs. Jelinek for the offer but explained that I remembered I had promised my mother I would go home and make sure Ben had lunch while she went to St. Mary's Hospital to visit a friend with breast cancer. I was only partly lying. Mom was going to visit her friend Suzanne at the hospital, but Ben was more than capable of preparing his own lunch.

I think Miranda knew I was making it up to be kind, and she went along, not wanting to embarrass her mother either. She walked me downstairs to the stoop. Before running back up to her mother, she told me I was sweet and kissed me quickly on the right cheek. I think I turned beet red, but none of the kids outside were even paying attention to us. I floated to the sidewalk and all the way home to River Street. Miranda Jelinek kissed <u>me</u>, Jack Sullivan, on the right cheek. Aside from that zom losing his foot, this turned out to be a really great day. Crazy, man.

## Sunday, October 1, 2017

Ben has been complaining all week about having to go back to school tomorrow. Too bad! All these kids in Hoboken are running around crazy unsupervised in the streets. No parent has the strength to set rules or discipline their kids anymore. Everyone knows death is around the corner. People often say, "Just let the kids have a little fun while they can." But something has to be done about it. When this zombie pandemic ends, if it ends, we're going to have a generation of children who can't read or write or do basic math.

The only person I told about Miranda's kiss was Tony. I don't want to spoil the experience by telling Jason or Kahil. They would just make jokes about it. Tony told me to take it slow and not act any differently than I would have if this had happened a year ago. He said that lots of adults in Hoboken are acting out because they're frightened and believe their lives are almost over. "End of the world sex," he called it. I appreciate the advice, maybe the same thing my dad would have said if he was here. I suppose that's partly why I told Tony in the first place, to get some fatherly advice.

But if the end is near do I want to die a virgin? I'm sure 14 is too young to be considering such things. Except, 14 is like 35 now. We have to cram a lot of living into what may turn out to be a very short period of time. When I think of Miranda, I imagine it is how Anne thought of Peter van Pels (named Peter van Daan in her diary). Her only chance for love maybe ever in her life, and she couldn't let it go by.

## Thursday, October 5, 2017

We've reached another full moon tonight. There it hangs, perfectly positioned over the Empire State Building. There are scientists and astronauts up there on the lunar surface, nine of them in total. What do they know about the present course of events on Earth? Are they watching us through some supersonic telescope? Do they see the hordes of zom destroying the world? Or have they turned their telescope off, maybe pointed it in another direction to see what new planets they can discover and populate? There is no reason for them to come back here.

At least there are those nine people who have escaped this spinning, rotting sphere. And another fourteen in the International Space Station. The remaining seven billion of us are returning to our caveman times. Well, those of us who haven't become zom. I wonder how many that is. We humans may prevail, but we'll be starting from scratch. The zom are our dinosaurs. We need an asteroid or ice age or biological fluke to come along and finish them off so we can begin the work of rebuilding. Of course, most of those things would finish us off, too.

I think about the Yellowstone Caldera, the supervolcano located in the northwest corner of Wyoming, erupting and putting us all out of our misery. When the volcano eventually erupts, as it will some day, one thousand miles of hot lava will spew across the United States and Canada, killing everything in its path. I learned this from a show about volcanoes on the National Geographic Channel. God, I miss television! Nothing else like it can make an empty room seem less empty and lonesome.

Since the zom are already dead, in the old sense of the word "dead", I wonder if they would just keep trudging through the boiling lava of the Yellowstone Caldera. Maybe we can only hope for our misery to end. Maybe the zom are now a permanent force in the universe, to be constantly "reborn" after the lava cools or the ice melts or whatever else that stops them in their tracks changes its form and allows them to be set free again.

Saturday, October 7, 2017

Miranda and I had scout duty this morning with Serena. I think Serena senses something has changed between me and Miranda. She asked me if everything was OK and said I seemed different this past week. I told her that I have good days and bad days like everyone else and this week has been the usual mixture of both. Miranda and I haven't discussed the kiss. I suppose it might not have meant the same thing to her as it did to me. She's very "New York" and a bit of a free spirit. I guess I should try to get some more time alone with her and see what happens.

Zom activity has intensified along the Observer barricade. Word has it that there is a merging of Manhattan zombies pouring out of the Holland Tunnel with hordes of Jersey and probably Pennsylvania zom finding their way here from the west. Too bad we can't capture and tag some of them like they do with migrating birds to see how far they travel and whether they always come back to the same spot.

The City Council has ordered that ammunition only be used for an actual breach of the barricades. We can't afford to use bullets on the packs of zom who drift aimlessly around no man's land. We also can't use bullets to shoot birds out of the sky for food either. Fish and rats and roof grown vegetables are pretty much our entire diet at this point. I think we're fortunate. There must be people out there trapped in isolated places, perhaps by themselves for all these months since the pandemic began. Once their food is gone, what can they do if the zom are crawling everywhere outside their hiding places?

We just sit in our scout tower and watch the parade below. All of us have become experts in zom behavior and evolution, because in less than a year they have begun to change. Not only are they physically more repulsive as they lose more skin, more flesh, more limbs and extremities. They seem to be traveling in larger and larger packs, sometimes several thousand at a time moving together like one organism with legs and arms, heads and torsos, intertwined. This may be the reason why they also appear lately to move more slowly. When you have 2,000 feet shuffling and galumphing along together it can be rather clumsy, like a mile wide rotting Snuffleupagus. Will their apparent "desire" to come together and form some new kind of creature be their ultimate undoing? They are accidentally ripping each other apart, yanking off arms and legs while trying to move as one.

I've never seen a rat king - the phenomenon where a number of rats become entangled at the tail, glued together by shit and blood and dirt, and continue to live and even thrive - but I think what we're seeing on the other side of the barricade is the dawn of the zombie rat king. The zom are covered in blood, filth and waste, which cements them together once their limbs and torsos become entwined. This world keeps getting more and more bizarre. The planet has become unrecognizable. Evolution, demented and mutant, thrust into high speed. That's what we have here now. Crazy, man. Just absolutely crazy.

*Monday, October 9, 2017*

I walked up and down Hudson Street this afternoon trying to kill time and not look stupid waiting for Miranda to
appear on her stoop. When she spotted me and called out
my name I pretended I was on my way home from visiting
Jason. She didn't seem to suspect that I was showing a little
bit of creepy stalker behavior. I asked her if she was on her
way to work a shift on the barricade. She said that she wasn't
scouting today and had decided to take a walk along the waterfront. I asked if she'd mind some company. She smiled
this beautiful, totally not phony smile and said that she'd
love my company. Miranda actually used the word "love" in
relation to something about me.

We walked the path through Stevens Park, corn as high as
an elephant's eye (I think I got that from a song?) growing
on each side of the path. It's part of the Hoboken Agricul-
tural Project. We came out of the corn stalks on Frank Sinatra Drive, across the street from my building, and turned
left, heading north past Castle Point Park along the water.
The howling from across the river was loud today, especially
loud for such a warm and sunny day. I wondered how many
zombie rat kings were trying to navigate the streets of Manhattan. But I didn't want the conversation to turn to zom.
That seems to be all people talk about any more.

Along the riverbank, about a hundred or so folks - an
equal mix of men, women and children - were doing laundry, whacking their clothes against the rocks in the surf

below the Hoboken Cove Boathouse. Well, by surf I mean those little waves you get in the Hudson now and then that we've always called the surf. Miranda was totally calm and at ease as we walked. I think it's just in her nature to be a tranquil person. I asked her about life before the arrival of Passenger Zero. I realized that I didn't know that much about her, other than that she and her mother fled Tribeca just in time.

She told me that her father was an investment banker who spent a lot of time in London, Paris and Brussels on business. The last Miranda knew, he was in London for a meeting. She talked to him early in the morning the day she left for Hoboken, during the last hours of international cell phone service. The United Kingdom was on lock down and London had not yet seen a zombie outbreak. But there were reports of possible zom activity coming from Cardiff, Wales as well as Bristol and Bath in the south of England. No more than me, Miranda hasn't a clue whether her father is alive or dead. London might be a giant British version of Fortress Hoboken. Or it might be a city of zombie rat kings. Another howling, stinking wasteland like New York. Despite my good intentions, I led us smack into another conversation about the zom. I suppose there's no getting around it.

We continued walking until we reached Elysian Park at the intersection of Sinatra Drive and Hudson Street. Tomatoes and other vegetables grew on every available patch of land. There's a plaque at Elysian Park that says it was the birthplace of baseball in 1846. Can you imagine Citi Field or Yankee Stadium today? Zom wandering the stands, tripping and falling over each other on to the field. If I was to go see a game now I would definitely want it to be on bat day. Whack open a few dozen zom skulls and give new meaning to the term "slugger". Wow, a sense of humor? Was afraid I'd lost that.

Miranda and I sat down on an unoccupied bench facing a black wrought iron fence with New York across the water on the other side. From the bench it appeared that Manhattan was imprisoned behind bars. It was nice to sit there with Miranda and not feel the need to speak. Neither of us said anything for at least fifteen minutes. Even though it was warm, some of the trees had already started to change colors. Eventually, she said, "This is the most beautiful day I've seen since I've been here."

I reached across the bench and took her hand in mine. She turned her head and smiled at me. We sat like that for at least half an hour, the soft skin of her hand the coolest thing I had ever felt. Strangely, my mind raced back to the girl I "killed", never to sit on a park bench and hold a boy's hand, or a girl's hand for that matter. I had to work at banishing her from my thoughts. I was there with Miranda. She and I were both alive and it felt the best. What's the point of living if you're constantly going to dwell on death and despair? This fall of 2017 might be all I get. Anne and Peter again. This is it. I am choosing to live, and today I am also choosing to be happy.

When we stood up from the bench I counted to five real fast and leaned in and kissed Miranda on the lips. Our mouths pressed together for three seconds, maybe four. The best three to four seconds of my life. We left Elysian Park and walked slowly along Hudson Street back to her building. People jammed the sidewalks as usual. Kids were everywhere. I didn't care.

Even with all those people bumping into us and the constant need to say "excuse me" every ten feet, I felt today like Miranda and I occupied our own private world. It was 1995 and we were young Clintonites (Dad always talked about how great the 1990s were) filled with hope and promise, eager to rush home and try out the internet for the first time. I felt today like anything is possible. That I have youth on my side and all the time in the world to live a full life. It couldn't have been further from reality. I know that. But it felt so perfect anyway. Crazy, man. Absolutely crazy. Crazy and wonderful at the same time.

Friday, October 13, 2017

That's right. Friday the 13th, the second one of the year. I know that any month that begins with the 1st on a Sunday has a Friday the 13th. Some years have three of them. I guess

I never paid them much attention in the past. But they seem especially weird this year. The one in January was when that zom burst into the Chechnyan Parliament on live international television and the world got its first pictures of something almost everyone on the planet would see again and again in the month to come before television disappeared.

This Friday the 13th was marked by a different event. A small boat drifted across the river early in the morning containing six hungry, writhing zom. The river lookouts missed the boat somehow, and it made land at Pier C Park - directly under my bedroom window - with all six zom coming ashore. I suppose it was inevitable that they would eventually penetrate Fortress Hoboken. Since it was barely dawn there was no one on the waterfront except the lookouts. The first shot woke me and Ben. We ran to the window in time to see the standoff, three lookouts with guns confronting six zom on Hoboken soil. Five of the zom were each hit square in the head and fell to the ground.

But they missed one, a female zom, and she made contact with one of the lookouts, biting into his right arm before she could be put down, too. The lookout who was bit stood and stared at his wound, the arm actually dangling off his shoulder, blood everywhere, while the other two lookouts just stared at him in shock. With his left arm he raised his gun to his head and pulled the trigger, falling to the ground a few feet from the six zom corpses. Ben ran to his bed and jumped under the covers. I looked out the window one last time and then went to him, climbing under the sheet since it was still too warm for a blanket. I told Ben about life on the moon one more time and eventually he fell asleep. I know the dreams the poor little guy had after witnessing his first zombie attack and human suicide, the same dreams we all have of being chased and caught over and over. Don't tell me Friday the 13$^{th}$ isn't an unlucky day.

## Wednesday, October 18, 2017

Mr. Rosen has disappeared more and more into his own private world these last few weeks. Mom and Lily are so good with him. He kept Mom going all those months when she couldn't even get out of bed some days and she has returned the favor. I know she worries about her own parents, my other faraway Grandma and Grandpa who live in Houston, Texas. Before we lost the internet I read blog posts and tweets about zom activity in New Orleans, Dallas, El Paso, Oklahoma City, Tucson, Phoenix, San Diego, and Los Angeles. The zom made it from Brazil to the Mexican border pretty quickly, and no electrified fence or border patrol could stop them from that point. There are probably pockets of people alive in the desert and mountains, but the southwest seemed to definitely be another zombie epicenter. Mom's sisters - Aunt Clare and Aunt Deirdre - lived in the Houston area, too, with their families. Is it possible any of them are still alive? Mom was especially close with Grandpa. I think when she takes care of Mr. Rosen she imagines taking care of her own father.

I watch Lily as she moves around the apartment, helping Mom with Mr. Rosen, sitting down with Ben and reviewing his homework, making a meal for all of us out of fresh herbs and a blue fish caught off Pier A. Then I think of her alone in a basement in New York, hiding from the zom, grieving Doug, wondering how his end came about. It makes me so sad to think of this beautiful person who has come to be such an important part of our family existing the way she did for so long, and in a way none of us have had to endure. Is my father still living like that? Afraid and possibly alone in constant danger. Even if he's gone, how many others suffer the life of Lily in that city? Why did human existence end up here for all of us? Today, I am most definitely angry at God, and I expect a whole lot of answers. Answers I bet I'm never going to get in this lifetime. I wish I had never vowed to not curse in this diary.

Thursday, October 19, 2017

I woke up this morning and Mom was sitting on the end of my bed. I knew what she was going to tell me before she said it. Mr. Rosen had died in his sleep during the night. We're all sad and miss him more than I can say, but I think it's great that there is still somewhere in this world where an old man can die peacefully in his bed surrounded by people who love him. Mr. Rosen may turn out to be the last human to have such a death. Mom said it's important to get Mr. Rosen "buried" right away since he was Jewish and that is part of their beliefs. You bury the person the day after they die and then the family sits Shiva, meaning for one week people come by the house to pay their respects. Not that anyone follows all these old rules at this point in the pandemic.

There were several funeral homes in Hoboken before everything happened. I think three in total. Funny, but a zombie apocalypse is never good for the funeral business. When someone dies in Hoboken now there is no embalming that takes place, no wake or viewing. There is just a short service at the end of Pier A before the person is buried at sea. Actually, they are dropped in the river to float out to the ocean. The town decided at the very beginning that our dead would not end up in the lime pit with the zom. If you die a human and don't reanimate then something resembling an old fashioned funeral has to take place. I think this is done for the sake of the living as much as for the dead.

Mr. Rosen is lying in his bed now covered up to his shoulders with a white sheet. He was never bit by a zom while he was alive, so from what we know about the virus he is not infected. It's safe for us to give his body some dignity. I went and sat with him for a while. Is it a stupid cliché to say he looked peaceful? The light streamed through the window during what was otherwise a cloudy day as I held Mr. Rosen's cold hand and talked in a real low voice to his spirit, which was probably still floating around the room. It was so nice knowing he wouldn't reanimate, that I could sit there and hold his hand and talk and not have to shoot him in the head.

We'll take him down to the waterfront in the morning. Tony said he would help us. Lily got someone to donate an Israeli flag with the Star of David so we can send Mr. Rosen out to sea properly wrapped. I wonder if Mr. Rosen was the last survivor of the Warsaw Ghetto and Treblinka? I guess it's possible that the Holocaust, along with everything else in human history, soon won't be remembered by anyone. The zom don't seem too big on honoring the past, or honoring anything for that matter.

## Friday, October 20, 2017

We "buried" Mr. Rosen early this morning. Just before we left the apartment with his body a note was delivered for Mom. Her friend Suzanne died of breast cancer yesterday as well, the same day as Mr. Rosen. Mom said it had been really hard on Suzanne in the end. The hospital does its best for people, but it is just not possible to treat sick people like in the before days. Mom says that what Suzanne needed in the end was morphine, which is no longer available. When she told us Suzanne had died, I became worried for Mom that all of this sudden loss would send her on another downward spiral. She says she is OK. Maybe there has been so much loss for her by now that she expects nothing but loss upon loss upon loss any more.

Tony got two guys from his floor, Rob and Danny, to volunteer to help us carry Mr. Rosen to the first floor. I remember Rob and Danny from before, both investment bankers in their mid twenties who used to work all the time and always talked on their cell phones in the elevator. When Hoboken sealed itself off from the world, Rob and Danny sealed themselves in their apartment with a trash bag full of marijuana that Danny bought using all the money in his checking account. Nobody really cares that they're stoned all the time. Everyone does what they have to in order to survive. But Mom won't let me hang out in their apartment, not that I'd want to. As much as I appreciate the smell of anything besides rotting flesh, marijuana smoke makes me nauseous. Besides, you can't be ready to fight the zom if you're stoned all the time. All zombie scouts take a pledge that we won't use any mind altering substances. The safety of Hoboken depends on us being alert and clear minded at every moment.

Stoned as they were, Rob and Danny took their role as pallbearers seriously and carried Mr. Rosen wrapped in the Israeli flag with great care. Mom, Lily, Ben, and I walked behind them with Ginger. Jason and Miranda showed up as we were leaving. Serena, Kahil and Peter had scout duty so they couldn't make it. Mrs. Adelman, an elderly neighbor friend of Mr. Rosen, also joined us. We walked as a group to Pier A, with Mr. Rosen hoisted up on Tony, Rob and Danny's shoulders once we were outside. The sky was dark, enormous gray clouds and an ocean of fog for Mr. Rosen's farewell. No rain, though, which we badly need. The few people we passed along the waterfront bowed their heads as we went by. People have a great respect for human dead these days. I think this is more than just relief that these dead have not reanimated. It's a way to acknowledge who we once were. And who we will be again someday.

When we reached the water's edge, the guys lowered Mr. Rosen to the ground so some words could be said. It was a good thing Mrs. Adelman was there. She was able to say the Kaddish, the Jewish prayer of mourning for the dead. I don't speak Hebrew so I didn't know what the words meant, but the sound of that prayer being recited by Mrs. Adelman was one of the most beautiful sounds I've ever heard in my life.

When she finished we all bowed our heads for a moment of silence. Then the guys lifted Mr. Rosen back into the air and dropped him off the end of the pier into the river. The current quickly carried him wrapped in the Israeli flag in the direction of the harbor and the Statue of Liberty. He didn't sink but kept floating, drifting further and further toward the Atlantic Ocean. Goodbye, Mr. Rosen! I will never forget you and the story you told me. If I survive this, if the human species survives this, I will make sure future generations know what happened to you and your family in Warsaw and Treblinka.

## Tuesday, October 31, 2017

Halloween is not something anyone feels like celebrating this year. There certainly won't be trick-or-treating for the kids or the annual parade down Washington Street, which is normally a big deal in this town. The idea of dressing up like ghosts and goblins seems a little too creepy while real ghouls are trying to penetrate the barricades. I can't believe that two years ago I actually dressed up with Ben and Dad and Uncle Matt as a family of zombies. We have photos from that Halloween, which I can't bring myself to look at now. I remember that Mom refused to join us in dressing up even though we all begged her and told her it was just for fun. Maybe she was the one who was truly in touch with what was coming. Maybe it was Mom who knew the future all along.

## Saturday, November 4, 2017

A full moon tonight. Ben and I tried again to locate the Moonbase Lunar Colony through Uncle Matt's telescope.

It has become a ritual for us whenever there is a full moon. As he searched the lunar surface, I told Ben stories of our future adventures skateboarding the moon's peaks and valleys. Ben seems to be missing Mr. Rosen more than any of us. He lost his friend, his replacement grandfather, and the best male role model he had. I tried to get him to talk about it, but when it comes to the death of Mr. Rosen, Ben just wants to be left alone. I understand that and won't force the subject.

I haven't written about our missing 23 for a while. Most people don't even mention them anymore. Tony still monitors the airwaves for a half hour twice every day, hoping to pick up a transmission from them. I think they're all dead. They must be dead. Otherwise, they would have gotten back to us by now. They're gone for good. Probably just 23 more zom roaming Manhattan. They left in summer and winter will soon be here. Last night the temperature dropped a whole lot, which made me realize how much time had gone by since they'd left. I became a little sad thinking about them. But it did feel great to need a blanket again after so many warm and uncomfortable nights.

Zom activity along Observer Highway has really picked up. One zombie rat king after another finds its way to us, rarely less than a hundred rotting torsos entwined together. The good thing about their tendency to become so entangled is that they move with much less ease and can't even begin to figure out how to penetrate the barricade like that.

We watch them from the tower with our binoculars, legs and arms and heads ripping off, one, then another, as they try to navigate the terrain, the packs of wild dogs always in tow.

Every now and then a zom approaches alone. If a zombie rat king is in the vicinity, the lone zom usually gets sucked into the larger organism. If no zombie rat king is around, the solo zom does its best to get to us, desperate to feed. Not much is left of them after almost a year, but what's there is as vicious and deadly as ever. Today I saw two lone zom - at this point male or female is impossible to determine - each just a maggot covered torso with no arms but two shriveled legs moving them forward. They had no facial features, no hair, nothing really to even suggest they were once human. We used to be able to tell who they might have been before by the clothing they wore, but most have now lost their pants and shirts and skirts and dresses, even their underwear.

When they reached the barricade, both these zom leapt on to the barbed wire. It almost seemed an act of suicide, but that couldn't be I realize. They became speared in multiple spots. The more they squirmed to get free, the more what little was left of them shredded into puppy chow for the dogs who weren't far behind. It took eight wild dogs just five minutes to finish them off. I have always loved dogs. They licked the bones of those zom clean while the zom were still squirming on the barbed wire. We may actually be seeing the beginning of the end. Winston Churchill would be pleased.

*Sunday, November 5, 2017*

I spent the entire day reading up on the roof. Mr. Rosen left an incredible library of books behind, which we have stacked all around the apartment. Kindles, Nooks and iPads are relics of the past. Thank God we never threw away all the paper books. My goal is to read everything before either I die or the last zom is reduced to puppy chow. Today was *To Kill a Mockingbird.* I would have read it in school this year with Mr. Chupka if things had been different. I wish Atticus Finch was my father and he was here with me and Ben helping us deal with life amidst the zom. Atticus would have seen their former humanity, just like Miranda. But he also wouldn't have hesitated to shoot each and every last one of them, putting them out of their misery like he did the rabid dog in the story.

I think the rabid dog was actually a symbol of racism, and Atticus shooting the dog was a metaphor for the stand he would take against racism later in the story when he defended Tom Robinson. But for me everything is a metaphor for zombies. I can't help it. The rabid dog, the crazed lynch mob, Mayella Ewell's lie about Tom, even Boo Radley. It's all zom to me. Unfortunately, my Boo Radley won't turn out to be misunderstood, lonely, harmless, and kind. The reality of the situation is that my Boo Radley can't wait to chew off my arm and any other body part it manages to sink its zom teeth into. Sadly, it won't turn out that I'm wrong about this as it did for Scout and Jem in the novel.

## Tuesday, November 7, 2017

Rain! Wonderful, constant, no-end-in-sight rain! After several dry weeks we need this day of downpours more than any other single thing. I'm looking out my bedroom window now, watching as it cuts in sideway paths across the river. Keep coming down! I helped empty the rooftop rain barrels this morning. I'm sure Manny is back up there now making certain we don't lose a drop. Thank you, Mr. Rosen and Suzanne, for sending the rain. We now just need you to send us a cure. If anyone can arrange that, Mr. Rosen can.

## Wednesday, November 8, 2017

Miranda and I went for a long walk today, roaming the boundaries of Hoboken as well as the length of Washington Street straight through the heart of town. We set out early this morning thinking we would try to get a complete lay-out of the land, see with our own eyes the status of life here amongst the living. Things have been declining at warp speed it seems all over the place, and today's observations confirmed that. I met Miranda at 8:00 a.m. on her stoop and we walked together to City Hall at Washington Street between Newark and 1st.

We started off our day with an "End is Near!" preacher on the corner of 1st and Washington screaming about the last days and Zechariah 14:12 - "And the Lord will send a plague on all the nations that fought against Jerusalem. Their people will become like walking corpses, their flesh rotting away. Their eyes will rot in their sockets, and their tongues will rot in their mouths." I looked the passage up later and was pretty freaked out to see that the Old Testament Book of Zechariah seemed to predict the zombie apocalypse. No surprise that there were at least half a dozen more Zechariah prophets the length of Washington Street.

The first five blocks of Washington were jam packed with merchants. Eight roasted rat vendors, an equal number of used book sellers (after all, what do people have to do for fun anymore but read?), numerous pigeon (with the ban on shooting I guess they were killed by slingshot) and fish hawkers, kids selling plastic jugs of water from the recent rain, and countless individual citizens trying to trade their valuables for nonperishable food and firewood. A diamond ring or rare painting is worthless in this new world. A fur coat may turn out to be handy depending on what kind of winter we have. But a can of tomato soup is priceless so long as you own a can opener. Most of the storefronts have been converted into residences so business usually takes place on the street now. Cars, buses and trucks are completely absent from town, but pedicabs, bicycles and other manually operated contraptions ride up and down Washington and the side streets all day long.

As we walked Washington from 1st to 14th, we noticed how thin every person had become. I spotted one man at 7th and Washington who I used to always see at church in the old days. He was really, really fat just a year ago, probably over three hundred pounds. Even he is heading toward the slim side now. Some people are so skinny they look like the concentration camp survivors in the black and white film footage taken by the allies after they liberated the camps at the end of World War II, which I saw one night last year on the History Channel. I wonder now if Anne's body was in the pile of skeleton corpses I saw in that movie.

Once we reached the end of Washington we turned left on 14th and headed to Madison, the western border of town. We walked the barricade that runs between Madison and Monroe, waiving at our fellow scouts who were occupying each tower along the route. When we reached Observer Highway we took a left and headed east toward the river. It is the Observer barricade that sees the greatest amount of zom activity given its closeness to Jersey City, the Holland Tunnel, the PATH entrance, and the highways and drawbridges that lead west through New Jersey to the rest of America. As usual, the moaning of zom could be heard from the other side as Miranda and I made our way east. The chorus of howling told me another zombie rat king had appeared without my needing to climb the tower and take a look.

At Pier A and the waterfront we headed north past the W Hotel, followed by my building and Stevens Tech. Sinatra Drive and Castle Point Park, which winds north from there, are always crowded with people seeking some relief from the overflowing tenements of town. Today was no exception. The sounds of a zom-occupied Manhattan are still disturbing, but the open air and clear views of the river offer a break to people trapped for almost a year in a one square mile town containing six times the population it was meant to hold. When we reached Maxwell Place, Miranda and I continued walking toward the piers at 13th and 14th Streets, the northern most points in Hoboken.

We stood at the end of the 14th Street Pier and stared across at New York. After a few moments of silence, Miranda looked at me and said, "I'm glad I met you, Jack Sullivan. I'm of course sorry all this happened, but it is why I met you. I guess you can be sorry about one thing and happy about another thing that are tied together. Liking the good thing I don't think means that you betray everyone affected by the bad thing."

I nodded my understanding and agreement to what she was saying. I hate the zom but I love Miranda, and the one thing wouldn't have happened without the other. It's up to us to make peace with that.

After walking the width and length of Hoboken today, I see what I already knew. This is an amazingly self-contained city, but a city hanging on by a thin thread. Hoboken was not designed to keep 250,000+ people going indefinitely, especially with no supplies ever arriving from the outside. Each day could be the day we are overrun by zom or the day we turn on each other. Suppose it takes another year or more for the zom threat to decrease enough for us to again attempt to venture out from town? How many will survive the year? It's a race against the calendar between us and them. One of us will outlast the other. I honestly don't know who will win.

## Monday, November 13, 2017

We actually had snow flurries today. Snow falling on Hoboken and it is barely the middle of November. Is Ben going to have his first real taste of winter? Lily was saying to Mom this morning that just because winters have been mild the past few years due to global warming doesn't mean a mini Ice Age can't be on the horizon. The polar ice caps have probably melted enough by now that the horrible winters some weather experts predicted might finally be here. If I understand it correctly, the Gulf Stream that warms Europe and the northeast of North America would be eliminated if enough ice from Greenland and the Arctic melts into the North Atlantic.

How we'll find enough wood to heat our way through the winter might turn out to be Hoboken's biggest challenge yet. Already we live without toilet paper. Most of us use our own personal designated rag (Ben and I call it our "shit rag" when Mom isn't listening) and lug our waste outside in a bucket to dump in the sewer. That humiliating reality we can endure and survive. But a winter without firewood, a winter without heat - that we couldn't survive.

## Thursday, November 16, 2017

Today the snow really came down, almost three inches. Kids were out in droves playing, snow balls flying in every direction. It was too soft for snowmen, but I have a feeling the snowman snow is coming. As I watched the fun from my bedroom window, I spotted a sight I hadn't seen in months - a boat approaching Hoboken. I looked through the telescope and saw that it was a small row boat containing a single occupant coming toward us from downtown Manhattan. I called out for Mom and Lily to come see. Ben was down on the waterfront playing with the other kids in the white stuff.

"It's definitely a survivor," Lily said after looking through the telescope. "I think a male. I'm going down to meet him."

I left the apartment with Lily. Mom stayed upstairs at my bedroom window following the survivor's progress through Uncle Matt's telescope. When Lily and I reached the playground on Pier C there was already a crowd assembled cheering the new arrival as he paddled toward shore. As he got closer I could tell that he was of Asian descent, and thinner even than any person in Hoboken. Lok Kwong turned out to be his name, 22 years old. He had lost everyone he ever knew to the zom and was shaking uncontrollably as he spit out his story.

He told us he spent six months trying to get from Chinatown to the West Side Highway, plodding and thinking and analyzing every angle, every possibility, everything that could go wrong if he tried to make his escape. All he dreamed of since the collapse of life in the city was getting to a boat and sailing up (or down) the Hudson River, away from the hordes of zom. He hadn't seen another survivor since early September when he spotted a teenage girl scavenging trash cans seconds before six zom came out of nowhere and descended on her, leaving nothing behind but a pile of bones when they finished. Then Lok collapsed in tears on the ground and didn't stop kissing the snow-covered pier until two members of the WDC gently escorted him away. The WDC have little work anymore. It's good to know that out there in the zom wilderness people are still finding ways to survive and reach us.

Saturday, November 18, 2017

I knew it was coming before it happened. Lily asked Mom if Lok could move in with us and stay in Mr. Rosen's room. The apartment has felt so empty since Mr. Rosen died. Lily thought that no one but her could really understand what Lok had been through all that time alone in Manhattan.

While Mom had some concerns about living with a strange man who might very well be insane from nearly a year battling the zom by himself, she ultimately agreed to Lily's request so long as Lok was given a full psychological exam at the hospital before moving in. She explained that as a single parent she had certain responsibilities to Ben and me to keep us safe. I never heard Mom refer to herself before as a single parent. Perhaps she is growing to accept finally that Dad is most likely dead. True, Lok is proof that there are people alive in Manhattan, but apparently there are not many of them. He may turn out to be the last person who escapes that city for the safety of Hoboken.

## Tuesday, November 21, 2017

Lok moved into Mr. Rosen's room today. He is quiet and obviously suffering from his experiences even more than Lily when she arrived. Mom called it post-traumatic stress disorder. I think Lok has been alone for so long under such difficult conditions that he doesn't know how to interact with other human beings any more. He looks down when you speak to him and says little in response to your questions. Lily sits with him a lot, telling him to take his time getting used to life with us.

In two days it will be Thanksgiving, and as in every other home in Hoboken the dinner this year won't be turkey (where would we get one?) but pigeon instead. The City Council authorized a pigeon kill on Sunday in honor of the day. A bird by any other name is still a bird, I suppose. All week I have found my mind wandering back to last year's Thanksgiving on that other planet called Earth where we used to live. Mom, Dad, Ben and I went into the city and had dinner with Uncle Matt and Jed at Uncle Matt's place on Cornelia Street. I think that day was the last time I saw poor Tolstoy. He spent the afternoon and evening curled up on the window sill, pretty much keeping to himself. If anyone could have survived many months alone without human contact it would have been that cat. Tolstoy was severely over weight so he had plenty of body fat to absorb if no one was around to feed him for a while. Hopefully, he's had access to mice and rats and can catch his own dinner.

Last Thanksgiving was the first time we all met Jed, who like I said before was a very nice guy. It was a big deal for Uncle Matt to host Thanksgiving since he had never prepared a holiday meal before. I think actually the fancy grocery store at 6th Avenue and 9th Street that Uncle Matt loved so much prepared most of the meal, but he really did figure out how to turn on his oven and roast a turkey. Mom was truly impressed by that. She kept congratulating him all evening. Memories like that of the old days grow dimmer and dimmer. It almost seems strange to me now to try and imagine that life again. I cannot get my mind around the idea of a world where the zom did not rise up and destroy civilization. You get used to that which you must. As Mr. Rosen used to say, the young figure out how to adapt and survive. It is what young people always do. It is why the human species has managed to survive insanely horrible things so many times throughout history. And we're doing it once more.

## Thursday, November 23, 2017

Snow fell again today while I spent the morning in the tower scouting with Serena and Jason. It was like the Macy's Thanksgiving Day Parade on the other side of the barricade. The zom kept coming, both individually and in groups. The rat kings were plentiful. Could they have somehow known what day it was? Were they lonesome for their old lives, all of them having spent last Thanksgiving somewhere else as functioning human beings? I'm sure it was my imagination but they seemed especially sad to me today, wandering in to each other, becoming entangled, moaning and howling as the snow descended on the last bits of their rotting flesh that still clung to their bones. The dogs don't seem to even bother following them any more, the meat no longer there to drop off as puppy chow. As I watched the parade through my binoculars I said to Jason and Serena, "We may be seeing their last hurrah."

After scout duty I headed home for our "traditional" pigeon dinner with all the trimmings. Mom and Lily did the best they could to make the meal special, even lighting some candles once it turned dark to allow us a few extra hours of light. Lok came out of his room and sat at the table with us for the first time. He apologized for being so solitary and nonsocial since his arrival. We told him not to worry about it, that we had been through it before with Lily and all of us understood. Much like Lily, Lok once he started talking couldn't stop. He told us everything that had happened to him since Passenger Zero landed at Kennedy Airport.

Chinatown is a large community but it is also an insular one. That is how Lok described it to us. The people in his building on Mott Street had begun bottling water and stockpiling food as soon as life in China experienced its quick domino collapse ending with the bloody Siege of Shanghai, which wasn't a siege at all. Just a two day desperate, hopeless attempt to fight off one billion zom. I think when China collapsed the world knew it was over, even if no one would or could admit it. The residents of Chinatown weren't caught off guard as much as other people when it happened in the United States because they accepted as true what had happened in their motherland. Much like Hoboken, the community mobilized and set up makeshift barricades along the boundaries of the neighborhood.

They existed well enough like that until one day in July that Lok said he would never forget as long as he lived. The zom had been pushing against the Chinatown barricades from the beginning, tens of thousands of them on a daily basis trying to get through and devour the inhabitants of Chinatown. That awful day in July they succeeded and burst through like water from a broken dam. It was brutal and over in a matter of minutes, Lok said. The survivors of the massacre fled in every direction. Lok found a basement under a grocery store on Canal Street that had a well-secured storage room. He would creep up to the building's rooftop now and then. Looking east, north and south, he saw hundreds of thousands of zom roaming the streets. Only west was clear of them in isolated patches.

When the snow came and his food ran out, Lok knew it was time to attempt an escape and head for the river. As he made his way there, the first few blocks were quiet. Then he reached Varick Street and had to outrun a pack of zom who all still had their legs. But he made it to the water and found a dinghy tied to one of the moored ferries. He untied the rope, climbed in the boat, and since he wasn't aware that the zom wouldn't follow him into the water, began to paddle with a piece of driftwood using every last ounce of his strength. He had no idea Hoboken was waiting for him on the other side. Welcome Lok! Happy Thanksgiving, indeed!!

## Saturday, November 25, 2017

Ben, Lily and I took Lok for a walk around Hoboken today. There was a light snowfall. There seems to always be a light snowfall lately. It is interesting to see Hoboken through the eyes of someone new. Lok was shocked to see what he called a vibrant community existing in a world that he thought was completely dead. He said he had no idea that we were here living as we do while he huddled for all those months alone in that basement storage room on Canal Street. When we asked him about Tudor City or any other large group of survivors in New York he said that he was not aware of any. I think Tudor City is gone like Chinatown.

Lok did tell us that as he ran toward the water he heard a hand full of survivors yell to him from windows here and there between Canal Street and the West Side Highway. Maybe a half a dozen different voices, both male and female. He couldn't stop for them. With the zom bearing down on him he had to keep running. But people were definitely up in those buildings. They are probably still there. How horrible for them!

Lily told Lok about her own experiences in the city. And about the 23 explorers who sailed from Hoboken in search of help. He knew nothing about them, never encountered anyone from Hoboken trapped inland away from their boat. As we walked along the waterfront with Manhattan across the river, Lok said that New York is a city teeming with zom, millions of them wandering up and down every side street and major avenue. When it was still hot they were less deadly during the day because they seemed to have trouble moving quickly in the heat. But now that winter was upon us again they would be back to how they were when this all first went down.

Of course, most of the zom are sporting less flesh at this point in the pandemic, so maybe clanking bones chasing after you might be easier to escape. One thing Lok was sure of - without a reliable source of food and water, he could not see anyone surviving for long in Manhattan. He had no idea how the other survivors could be alive up in those buildings. Rain water, rodents, cockroaches, scavenged supplies, he supposed. The thought of people trapped and living like New Yorkers makes me feel ashamed of myself when I complain about our life in Hoboken.

*Wednesday, November 29, 2017*

Four inches of snow last night and December is still two days away. I look across the river at night and think about those men and women who screamed at Lok. Were they begging for help or asking if he needed help from them? Were they yelling at him to run to their downstairs door because they had plenty of food and water and could take in another survivor? I doubt it. They probably each saw a man running by their building at a point where they had been alone for weeks, maybe months. They cried out with no goal in mind other than to connect with another person at a time when they thought maybe they were the last man or woman alive.

I feel haunted by those people even though they probably aren't ghosts yet. I know how scared I get at night and it upsets me to think of anyone ever getting more scared than that. I would be terrified more than anything I know if I were one of them. Eleven months into the zombie pandemic and they have no community, no help, no opportunity to go outside and walk down the street and enjoy a beautiful day. Just sitting there alone waiting for the end to come. Trapped like Anne in their attics, but without Miep Gies and the other helpers coming with food.

## Sunday, December 3, 2017

A full moon tonight. This time last year the Empire State Building was lit up in red and green for the holiday season. This year there is nothing but blackness under the moonlight. I think the fact that Christmastime is here has made everyone even more depressed than they were already. And as we get closer to the 25th the depression is just going to increase. I think that this time of year makes us more aware of all we've lost during the last twelve months. Mom seems to be sinking into another depression and I worry since Mr. Rosen is no longer here to help her through it.

There are not going to be any Christmas trees this year, no sidewalk Santas, no lights or tinsel or decorations. Several churches, Catholic and Protestant, have set up outdoor manger scenes. Otherwise, there are no public displays of Christmas. Children tell each other that Santa Claus won't be able to ride in his sleigh and bring presents this year because of the zom. He is safe up at the North Pole with Mrs. Claus and the elves and reindeer waiting for all this to end. Next year he will be back. We invent new stories when we need them. Or change the stories we already have to fit our present situation.

The cold temperatures are creating heating problems for everyone. People are hoarding furniture, trees limbs and branches - lumber obtained from just about anywhere. Most stairs no longer have banisters and any wood not needed to keep a structure standing has been taken. Everyone wears six layers of clothing all the time. We have no fireplace in our apartment so we stay bundled up even when inside. There is a fireplace in the recreation room down on the fourth floor where people from the building are always hanging out. Scout duty has been complicated by the cold, too. It's difficult to endure four hour shifts in the lookout towers, especially at night when the wind blows so cold it cuts through you like a thousand knives.

The zom keep stumbling their way to the barricade along Observer Highway, though I am happy to report they are fewer in number. None of them are wearing clothing at this point after eleven months of dragging around their rotting limbs and torsos. They don't appear to feel the cold and are actually more coordinated than they were in the heat of summer. Strange how they are affected by one extreme and not the other. While there are not as many of them, and the zombie rat kings seem to have broken into smaller pieces of intertwined flesh and bone, the ones who are wandering about in no man's land are no less vicious and deadly than they were when this all began. They stare up at us in the lookout towers (when they have something resembling eyes in their sockets, that is) with the same bewildered expressions as ever. Operating on instinct alone, they are motivated only by their desire to feed. Some things never change.

## Monday, December 11, 2017

I had no motivation to write this past week. So I read instead. First *The Hunger Games* and then *The Book Thief*, both borrowed from Serena. I loved *The Hunger Games* and need to try and get my hands on the two sequels. When Katniss volunteered as tribute at the reaping to save her sister Prim, I could relate. I would definitely fight in the Hunger Games if it meant saving Ben. And it was so cool in the story how the adults threw everything on the shoulders of the kids. Because, really, isn't that how it always is? The likes of me and Katniss have to figure out how to save the day, time and time again. Save ourselves, save our parents, save our siblings. If it wasn't for us, the rest wouldn't make it.

I liked *The Book Thief* for different reasons. First, it was narrated by Death and took place in Nazi Germany. If ever it was appropriate that Death showed up in a place and told the story, it was Germany in the 1930s and 40s. Until, that is, here now in Hoboken I suppose. It would probably make sense for Death to narrate the story of the zom. But even though Death narrated *The Book Thief*, the story was really about life and how reading books can sometimes save a person during the darkest of days.

I didn't love Liesel Meminger the way I loved Katniss Everdeen, but I don't think I was supposed to. Liesel wasn't written to be a great hero (I guess it should be heroine) like Katniss. Liesel was an ordinary, mostly kind and thoughtful, dorky girl who found herself living in the worst of times and she did what she could to cope. She stole books and learned how to read them. I never imagined that books would become so important to me. Because like I said before, books are all we have left to take our minds off the zom.

Wednesday, December 13, 2017

Life has been completely reduced to hunger and cold and darkness. There is nothing else left to experience. I thought that by now help would have arrived, that we would have made contact with some military or scientific group working to end the pandemic. But I guess it is just us here in Hoboken. We are the last ones left. There has been an increase in deaths this past month due to illness and, sadly, suicide, though the suicides are almost always people over the age of forty. As Mr. Rosen said, the young adapt better.

It's hard for desperate, hungry, cold, frightened people to go on. They don't fear the zom any more as much as life continuing like this for an entire winter, a winter that I don't think many will survive. Tony told me that he saw a man and woman the other day jump from the top floor of the W Hotel while they held hands. Splat! Both gone. The end. No one thinks less of people who make this choice. Even if we ourselves would never do it, we understand.

Miranda is worried about her mother. Mrs. Jelinek has stopped getting out of bed, just like Mom on her bad days. What are we going to do? Do we sit in this one square mile and wait for the end to arrive? I'm afraid it will be very slow in coming and there will be a lot of suffering first. My thoughts race back to those poor people in the buildings in New York who shouted to Lok as he ran by. Are they still alive? Is there any chance we the humans will outlast the zom? Or is Earth destined to become the sole property of zombies? I would have preferred Planet of the Apes to Planet of the Zom. But I didn't get a say in any of this.

## Thursday, December 14, 2017

A new concern here in Hoboken is typhus, the same thing that killed Anne Frank. There have been thirtysomething cases on the west side of town in the Projects, and half of those people have died already. It will only get worse as the winter goes on. It's caused by yet another parasite, Rickettsiae, spread from person to person by lice and fleas in overcrowded, unsanitary conditions like we are experiencing. Without the proper antibiotics, the disease proves fatal for many people, and we don't have enough antibiotics in Hoboken. Maybe it won't be the zom who get us in the end. How funny if it turns out to be a different parasite - Rickettsiae - that kills off the population of this town. The zom will pour through the barricades eventually, only to find a quarter million corpses infected with typhus on the other side. As many of the adults say, the world ends not with a bang but a whimper. Crazy, man.

## Saturday, December 16, 2017

Thirtysomething cases of typhus has risen to five hundred and thirstysomething cases in just a few days. Since symptoms first appear within seven to fourteen days after exposure, the number may go up big time. Everyone is petrified, watching for signs of fever, headache, muscle pain, rash, and fatigue in themselves and their friends and family members. I find myself constantly raising the back of my hand to my forehead to see if I'm hot.

Life in the lookout tower continues to be difficult. There are less zom every day but they still number in the hundreds. At the peak we were seeing thousands every day wandering no man's land on the other side of the barricade. The hundreds we are seeing now are severely rotted and none appear to have all their limbs and extremities attached. Many can only drag their decayed, decomposing bodies along the ground. Mouths chomping at nothing except the putrid, cold air, the zom still seem eager to feed. We are not willing to give them the chance.

## Tuesday, December 19, 2017

Five hundred cases of typhus has turned into over one thousand cases, and close to a hundred people have died so far. The zom hover along the barricades, stumbling about, dragging what little is left of each of them, appearing to wait for all of us to keel over on this side of the wall. I imagine they would enjoy munching on our 250,000+ corpses so long as we weren't infected with the zom virus before we died. It has become a nightmarish waiting game. And just when you think this whole thing can't possibly get any worse - wham, a typhus epidemic!

While on scout duty today I saw two zom in the distance, alone away from the crowd that drifted close to the barricade. Through my binoculars I could see that one of them was still wearing a necktie, though his shirt had been ripped off. The other was maybe also a guy. The one without a necktie collapsed to the ground and stopped moving. The first zom, the one with a necktie, appeared to grab what was left of his friend to try and pull him to his feet. Maybe it just looked like that was happening from far away in the tower. Usually the zom act completely indifferent toward each other. They are total narcissists. But here were zom almost taking care of each other. It reminded me of the female zom with her carriage full of zombie toddlers so many months ago.

Then my mind raced to who these two zom might have been when they were still human. Was this Dad and Uncle Matt? Dad had a necktie on that last day, though his wasn't saturated with dried blood when he left the apartment. I'm pretty sure he wore a green tie that morning, but all the blood made it impossible to tell what color this tie had once been. If this was really Dad and Uncle Matt after almost a year of their flesh rotting, roaming the zombie wilderness, and somehow making it back to Hoboken, they were sticking together as brothers until the end.

The two zom never approached the barricade. Once the one without a necktie managed to stand again, they shuffled off away from the pack heading south and west. I followed them until they were both just a speck on the horizon. It was sad to watch them disappear. Even if it wasn't Dad and Uncle Matt, these two guys had been somebody's something. Fathers or husbands or sons or uncles or friends. They had both meant something to someone somewhere. I thought about them for the entire rest of the day. And I thought about them as human beings, not as zom.

## Thursday, December 21, 2017

Miranda's mother became ill today with symptoms of typhus. It's a story repeating itself all over town. Miranda can't stay with her mother in their small apartment until she recovers (most people mean "if she recovers", but they of course don't come out and say it). Mom has said Miranda can stay with us and sleep in Lily's nook; Lily will sleep with Mom in her room. I can tell that Miranda is worried about her mother. She has no idea if her father is still alive. Her mother is all she has left in the world.

After dinner we went up on the roof to have a look at the stars. It was a cold evening but clear. Miranda and I stared at the nighttime sky for half an hour, maybe longer, standing close together to stay warm. I showed her the Constellation Anne Frank and told her how Tony and I named it. She liked the name. Miranda said she often thought of Anne during her time here in Hoboken, how she might have confronted her plight and the threat of the zom. Anne Frank would have made one fierce zombie scout!

I shared with Miranda that I had all the same thoughts about Anne as she did, and how I wrote in this diary primarily because of her. From across the river we could hear the guttural moaning, but it wasn't difficult to tell that the howling was much less than even a month ago. The zom are running out of steam. A walking corpse may have an expiration date of one year. Or so we can only hope.

## Thursday, December 21, 2017

I stood in the lookout tower this morning with Serena and Jason staring at no man's land. The usual parade of skeletons shuffled by. Then out of nowhere a half dozen mostly in tact zom came charging toward us. They must have only recently crossed over from human. Barely rotting, strong and fast, they climbed on top of the skeletons, and each other, trying to scale the barricade. We opened fire. Despite hitting most of them, one somehow made it over, a big guy with a beard in a blue and green plaid lumberjack shirt. I never saw a zom manage to fly over the barricade like that before. And it only takes one.

Dripping blood from his mouth as he landed smack on his head, he was back on his feet in a second. I fired at him but missed as he slipped on the ice and went down again.

People roaming on our side of the barricade screamed and ran for cover. Serena took a shot at the zom just as he lunged for a small raggedy child frozen in place with fear. She got him. One bullet through the skull, penetrating the cerebral cortex. Without question the best shot of any of us, Serena saved the life of that five year old boy today. She probably saved all of us. Hoboken would have been done for if she had missed as I did.

It happened so quickly. I've never before seen a zom as strong and fast as this guy, and I've seen some strong and fast zom. We were all standing there shaking once he was finally "killed". The poor little boy burst out crying as the zombie lay motionless at his feet. A man ran to him and scooped him up, probably his father, and carried the boy away as he tried to console him. Those half dozen new zom show that there are people out there who have successfully survived for almost a year but remain very much in danger. I wonder where they hid all this time and how their end came about. This is far from over. New zom are in fact still being created out of us, the last of the sad, scared, worn out humans. Crazy, man.

This afternoon I needed to escape. My only option was to rummage through the stacks of books in my room and find something good to read. I've collected a lot of books this year, mostly thanks to Mr. Rosen, but also from other people. I decided on one Miranda gave me, *Looking for Alaska*, a sort of *The Catcher in the Rye* type story from 2005 set in an Alabama boarding school. Miranda said I would like the characters - Pudge, Alaska, the Colonel. She was right. How could you not like Miles "Pudge" Halter and his search for the "Great Perhaps"? I wanted my own "Great Perhaps", but what I got instead was this lousy zombie apocalypse. I suppose that is my "Great Perhaps". Still, I can't help thinking there was this other life that was meant to happen to me. Oh well. Doesn't matter now.

## Friday, December 22, 2017

More snow today. Mrs. Jelinek's condition got worse. Mom and Lily went over to take care of her. Though I'm happy that she found a reason to get out of bed, I am worried about Mom. Suppose she becomes infected, too. I can't lose both parents. What would Ben and I do if we were left completely alone in the world? Mom says I shouldn't worry, that she and Lily know what precautions to take. Besides, it made Miranda feel a lot better knowing that her mother wouldn't be left alone in their apartment without anyone to take care of her. I could not deny Miranda the look of being at peace that came over her face when Mom announced she was heading to see Mrs. Jelinek.

Funny, nobody talks about Christmas. We acknowledged Memorial Day, the 4th of July, the Anniversary of 9/11, even made an attempt at Thanksgiving. But Christmas everybody is pretending doesn't exist. It's not three days away as far as any of us are concerned. Santa hasn't been watching who's been naughty and who's been nice. The rat on a stick guys aren't advertising pre-Christmas sales. That world is gone. Christmas is gone. It is an old memory - a vestige I think they call it - of a bygone era. The only thing we have in Hoboken to suggest it's Christmas is the snow, the constantly falling snow.

I miss Christmas in many ways, but I must admit that I also don't care. How can you care about holidays that are no more when you live in a world that is no more? 2017 has been the worst year ever. Period. No question about it. In 2018 we either all die or the tide turns and we find a way out. Back maybe to something like the old world. Back to being normal. Except normal - I think - is dead forever. At least, for the rest of my lifetime.


## Saturday, December 23, 2017

The Blizzard of 2017 is here. We don't need a weather forecast to tell us. There are no more weather forecasts. We look up. We see the snow falling. It's intense. It doesn't let up. It's a snow storm. That's how we know we're having a blizzard. I can't imagine now having a man or woman appear on a screen in your living room to tell you what the weather will be for the next ten days.

The days of being told not just what will happen with the weather, but what to wear, what to see, what to buy, what to think, those days are gone. What's funny is that the snow doesn't care. The snow has no idea, doesn't know zom from human from dog. The snow falls, plain and simple. The snow will fall in the future, as well, when all this sadness and fear and death has become the awful, brutal past. But today it falls on me in this world. The awful, brutal present.

I was just down on the waterfront with Ben, Miranda, Lily, and Lok. The snow is thick and falling hard. Everyone's eye lashes were coated white almost as soon as we walked outside. Miranda managed a smile when Lok surprised Ben with a snowball, and then some of Ben's friends jumped into the fight to help Ben retaliate. Lily immediately took up sides with Lok. I stood on the side lines with Miranda, aware that her mind was most likely elsewhere. Mom said that Mrs. Jelinek is really sick and it could turn out either way. Miranda understands. She told Mom that she wants to help in the care of her mother, no matter the risk. Mom promised that she would try to get Mrs. Jelinek to agree when she went to see her today.

I'm looking out the window now and the snow is falling even harder than when we were outside. This much snow must be a good thing. The higher the drifts the more difficult it will be for the zom to move around. God bless the cold, wonderful snow, friend of man and foe of zom. I better bundle up for scout duty. Today will be a tough one in the tower.

I arrived home from scout duty as Mom was returning from taking care of Mrs. Jelinek. Lily was leaving to replace her. Mom told Miranda that her mother had agreed to let Miranda spend Christmas Day with her at their apartment. After four hours in the tower with Serena and Jason, I needed to go to my room, take off my wet clothes, and wrap several blankets around me until my teeth stopped chattering.

We estimate that over two feet of snow fell in the past twenty-four hours. It did have a huge effect on the zom. As they trudged and stumbled along the other side of the barricade, howling at a noticeably lower pitch as if their strength was leaving them, the snow stopped many of them in their tracks. For a while, whiteout conditions made it impossible to even see the zom, which meant we had to guard the barricade from the ground as well. Extra scouts were called to duty for this task. If we missed even one zom finding its way into Hoboken, no one would make it alive to Christmas morning. We don't ever want another close call, another zom bearing down on one of our children.

As the storm let up and visibility improved we could begin to make out figures stranded waist deep in the snow. The wind blew so hard that some of the zom were covered up to the top of their heads. Or in most cases, skulls. They looked like snowmen come to life since there was still movement under the drifts. That is our new Christmas caroling this year, the sound of zom moaning in the snow. As the moaning weakens, we may end up with a silent night after all.

## Sunday, December 24, 2017

"Oh, holy night. The zom are slowly dying. . . ." I know, that's lame. But it's the best I could do for a contemporary Christmas carol. This is the antithesis (another Lily word) of every Christmas Eve past. I promised Mom that I would attend Midnight Mass with her. Actually, the service is at 7:00 p.m. since people don't want to be roaming around Hoboken when it's real late in the pitch black of night. But it's still being called Midnight Mass. I want to be clear that this is not any desperate attempt on my part to capture a little of the old Christmas spirit. I could care less about the old Christmas spirit. This is my present to Mom. She doesn't want to go to Mass alone. Not tonight. I need to do this for her. Oh, holy night. . . . Please, God, help us.

It's 11:00 p.m. and I'm turning in for the night. No need to leave cookies and milk for Santa this year, or carrots for the reindeer. Ben and I insisted we do it every year when we were kids, and Mom always gave up after arguing that the reindeer had eaten plenty of carrots - "at every house since Australia", she would say - by the time they got to Hoboken.

We always made Christmas Eve the big celebration in our family. Uncle Matt would come over, usually with a friend or two, and Grandma when she was still alive would spend the night. We ate mozzarella, prosciutto, red peppers, and sundried tomatoes. Dad made his signature pigs-in-a-blanket. Uncle Matt always brought Mom a box of chocolate covered pretzels from this amazing place in the Village. Grandma drank scotch, which Dad always got special for her. The Christmas tree was set up in the corner of the living room. Mom had a talent for choosing a tree each year that was perfect, tall and full, but not too full that you couldn't properly hang the ornaments.

I stared at the empty corner all day - where the tree should have been - until we left for Mass. The only light in the apartment since darkness fell were two candles and a flashlight we turned on and off once in a while. We didn't even bother to drag the boxes of holiday decorations from the storage space in the basement this year. Mom said we would do Christmas the right way again maybe next year, once this horror was finally over. I didn't have the heart to tell Mom I think our old time Christmases are permanently a thing of the past.

Miranda attended Mass with Mom and me. Lily was with Mrs. Jelinek for the night and Ben stayed home with Lok. Mom doesn't want Ben out too much in crowds since young kids are a lot of the typhus victims. Normally people don't roam around the streets of Hoboken after dark, especially in winter. Working street lamps don't exist anymore. We carried the flash light with us to shine a path through the snow between our building and church. When we arrived at Our Lady of Grace the pews were already packed with people, and candles lit around the altar gave the place a strange beauty.

During the service children reenacted the Nativity, playing everything from angels to shepherds to goats and camels. There was even a real baby to play Jesus. I looked around the church as Father Murphy read from the Gospel of Luke. The children up on the altar stumbled about in the straw, bumping into each other as Father Murphy heralded the good news, "For unto you is born this day in the city of David a Savior, who is Christ the Lord."

Each face in the church, each worn out, older than normal looking face had a smile on it. They looked as if their problems had eased. They looked like it was Christmas. To quote from a different kind of scripture, "Every Who down in Whoville, the tall and the small. . . ." That's what it reminded me of, those Whos in Doctor Seuss understanding that the Grinch had stolen the commercial parts of Christmas, but believing that Christmas was truly about something other than what they had lost.

I sat between Miranda and Mom during the Mass in a pew so crowded I had no choice but be pressed tight against both of them. Miranda seemed hypnotized by the service. She isn't Catholic and had never been to Mass before. Her

151

dad is Jewish and her mom is Buddhist. I think Miranda said Mrs. Jelinek was raised Presbyterian. Anyway, as she watched the children act out the Nativity Story, I saw Miranda's face relax a bit for the first time since her mother became sick. Mom sat there smiling at how the youngest kids played their roles with great seriousness. It was the best to see Mom smile.

Father Murphy gave a sermon about this being the most difficult Christmas in the history of humanity, but that we would find a way through it together to better days. Mom started mumbling a prayer to herself at this point. In her mind this is all a horrible, tragic, temporary scene in an otherwise wonderful life. I, however, think this is the way things are going to be forever more. Even if the zom all expire or wear out or crumble to dust, that old world has been destroyed and we have to begin anew. From scratch. There is no going back. Merry Christmas, Hoboken. And to borrow from Charles Dickens - just before *Looking for Alaska* I read both *Great Expectations* and *A Christmas Carol* - I suppose I should conclude this entry by saying, "God bless us, every one!"

## Monday, December 25, 2017

Christmas morning and I'm off to the barricade. Miranda is heading over with Mom to spend the day with Mrs.

Jelinek. When we woke up this morning there were five wrapped presents on the kitchen table for Ben, me, Lily, Miranda, and Lok. Mom had to have Christmas morning. She gave Lily a half-filled bottle of her best perfume and one of Grandma's brooches, the one shaped like a Christmas tree. She gave Miranda an antique comb from the 1920s ("Art Deco" she said) that belonged to her Great Aunt Dot and a small corked bottle containing dirt from Yasgur's Farm in Bethel, New York, scooped up by her Aunt Chloe at Woodstock. Miranda was really impressed by the dirt. Like I said before, she would have made a great hippie. Mom gave Lok an autographed first edition of Ernest Hemingway's *For Whom the Bell Tolls* that belonged to Mr. Rosen. A gloomy choice I thought based on the title, but Lok loved it.

Mom gave Ben one of Dad's watches, a diver's watch with a silver metal clasp band. And she gave me another of Dad's watches, a vintage Omega Seamaster with a white face and black leather band. I thought it was kind of wonderful, even if it wasn't on purpose, that Mom gave both Ben and me the gift of time. Ginger also received a gift, a package of cigar-shaped rawhide bones that Mom purchased from one of the vendors on Washington Street months ago, hiding them away until today. Mom made Christmas morning special, just as she had done every Christmas morning since I was a little kid.

It was a tough day with the zom. They seemed even more sad than they did on Thanksgiving, throwing their boney limbs around, bits of flesh still dropping off. Though not a dog in sight. All of them were covered in snow, icicles forming off whatever body parts remained. The icicles actually made them a little less disgusting to look at. If you squinted they sort of resembled skeletal versions of Snow Miser from the old Christmas special, *The Year Without a Santa Claus*.

Then there was the guttural moaning. Serena called it mournful, and she is not one usually to sympathize with the zom. I think the end is near for them. I don't know how long it will take, and I don't know what it means for us. Are there even more new zom out there making their way to Hoboken, not as rotted and putrid as these? Could this nightmare really be over by springtime? I don't know what to think, what to hope for. Because what I really want is my old life back. But that will never happen. I know that. It takes a lot of guts to stare reality in the face and say, "OK, I can accept you." I'm trying to do that. We'll see if I succeed.

Wednesday, December 27, 2017

Mrs. Jelinek died this morning. Miranda and Mom and Lily were with her. I don't know what to say to Miranda. What could possibly come out of my mouth that would equal the loss of the only mother she will ever have. She is in Mom's room now sleeping. I wish I could go in there and hold her. When she came back to the apartment with Mom and Lily, I hugged her and said I was sorry. She squeezed me tight and said thank you. Then she walked into Mom's room and shut the door. Mom went in after her and didn't come out for an hour and a half, warning us when she exited the room to "leave Miranda be for now".

I realize that hundreds have died of typhus in Hoboken since the epidemic began, but this death is raw and biting and endlessly sad. It's gotten under my skin and burrowed straight to my heart. Poor Miranda. Could her father possibly still be alive? I think now I want Mr. Jelinek to return even more than my own father because if he doesn't Miranda will be totally, completely alone in life. And it hurts me to think about her having so much loss.

## Thursday, December 28, 2017

We "buried" Mrs. Jelinek this morning after an informal service at her apartment. Miranda spoke about her mother before we carried Mrs. Jelinek down to Pier A, everything from how she loved the old HBO series *Sex and the City* so much that she named Miranda after her favorite character, to how brave and clear-headed she was the day she made Miranda pack a bag and get on the PATH train for Hoboken. Mrs. Jelinek figured out the quickest, safest, easiest way to flee Manhattan and give her daughter and herself a fighting chance. She knew the city would become a death trap and decided whatever happened in New Jersey would be preferable to seeing New York go the way of Paris and Shanghai and so many other cities.

Lok, Tony, Rob, and Danny carried Mrs. Jelinek wrapped in a white bed sheet from the brownstone on Hudson Street to the river. At the end of Pier A, Mom said a few words. She understood Mrs. Jelinek - Amy, she called her - as a mother in the same situation as her. Actually, Amy's situation was worse, Mom said, because she had lost her home, too. Mom had the luxury of still living in her own apartment. Mom then looked at Miranda and said, "Amy's courage and common sense the morning they fled Manhattan kept her greatest achievement alive, the amazing, astonishing daughter she raised into an exceptional young woman."

After Miranda said goodbye to her mother, the guys dropped Amy's covered body into the icy December water. That was it. She drifted away toward the ocean with the fast moving current. The look on Miranda's face as her mother's body floated away was beyond sad. They haven't invented the word yet for that look on Miranda's face. Those tears streaming down her cheeks broke my heart. It was another moment I will never forget as long as I live. There are too many of those moments now. I am all full when it comes to bad memories.

## Sunday, December 31, 2017

New Year's Eve, finally! 2018 is here at last. We made it. This godforsaken, lousy year, this blight on human existence - 2017, the worst year ever - has come to a conclusion. I'll take whatever comes next without complaint. It can't get any f-ing worse, and I know I promised no more cursing - at least, I think I promised that - but any shit that comes our way, any new mutation in our species, can only be an improvement over the zom.

Miranda has been understandably quiet since her mother died. She sits in the living room looking out the window toward Manhattan, probably thinking about her old life there. I imagine she is missing her father now as well as grieving for her mother. I am at a loss as to what to say to her. We have both lost our fathers and know what that is like. But I think losing your mother is worse, the worst thing that could happen. I can't imagine losing Mom. It was difficult in the beginning and I resented her depression in the face of our new reality. I didn't want to have to take care of her along with everything else I had to face. But she has changed and adapted, rising to the occasion, especially in nursing Mrs. Jelinek.

I think back to before Mr. Rosen came to live with us, when Mom was in really bad shape, even more than I was willing to admit. If it had not been for Mr. Rosen I would not have known how to care for her. Without him and his unique understanding of her based on his experience with his own mother, Mom would not have gotten better. It would kill me if she fell again into that deep pit of despair, and it would destroy me if she was no longer here in life with us. I guess I can live without Dad because I have proven I can. Mom is another story. She has always been the glue that holds this family together. I see that now.

## Monday, January 1, 2018

Happy New Year! There were times when I did not think I would live to write the year 2018 in these pages, but here I am and I'm writing 2018. I spent New Year's Eve on the barricade. Miranda insisted on joining me and Jason and Serena for our midnight scout duty. Hoboken must be guarded from the zom twenty-four hours a day, seven days a week, and there are no holiday exceptions. At 11:00 p.m. the four of us got settled in for the shift until 1:00 a.m. The full moon reflected off the blanket of snow that covered Hoboken and the world beyond. The frigid cold and snow has meant scout duty is reduced to two hour shifts, which - trust me - is more than enough time to be outside on a bitter cold night, even with the corrugated metal roofs constructed over each lookout tower.

As the snow fell yet again, accumulating in drifts against both sides of the barricade, the zom continued their parade. Given the numbers, it appeared there had been a recent surge either from the west or from the Holland Tunnel or both. Serena said it reminded her of New Year's Eve in Times Square, minus the crazy hats and noise makers and confetti, of course. They trudged and crawled through the snow, not a single one still wholly intact. Around 11:30 p.m. the party shifted into high gear as a zombie rat king appeared on the horizon. Hundreds upon hundreds of intertwined zom moved together toward Hoboken, however slowly and lugubriously (Miranda's word for them, and I think a good description). 2017 had been their year and it was almost over. They appeared mournful because that is how we saw them, struggling to exist as they froze in place, bony arms snapping off their naked torsos. From the few who still had arms left, that is.

Thirty seconds before midnight we began to count down. On reaching ten our joy and enthusiasm felt as real as any other New Year's Eve. At midnight I kissed Miranda on the lips. Her mouth was warm, her skin soft and cold when I touched my hand to her cheek. Jason found his balls, frozen as they were, and leaned in to kiss Serena. She let him. But the romance couldn't last for long. The four of us quickly turned our attention back to the zom.

About ten feet from the barricade, the zombie rat king stopped moving. Though its countless limbs and torsos and heads kept writhing and twisting, the zombie rat king itself remained in that same position for the next hour as the blizzard continued with increasing intensity and the drifts kept the zom from approaching further. We watched the zom disappear under fields and mountains of snow, and there they remained for the rest of the night, the moon reflecting off their whitened figures dotting the landscape. The zombie rat king became like Mount Everest, or the Matterhorn. You could have skied down its snow covered slope.

## Thursday, January 4, 2018

The sun came out today and the temperature reached almost fifty degrees. It felt like that glimmer of springtime you get once or twice during really cold winters, which inspires everyone to carry on. We noticed the zom beginning to thaw as the snow melted around them. They appeared to be emerging from the drifts even more rotted than before, if that's possible. Many are complete skeletons, as if snowmen had been dissected and only their bones remained.

Weird that the bacteria that form on any corpse and devour it have been doing the same to the zom. They wanted to devour us but their own bacteria are devouring them first. Their skeletons still pose a danger, however, jaws chomping and hands - when they have hands - clawing at the air. These guys don't give up. But I'd rather have to take on a crazy skeleton any day than a running, howling, vicious zombie. I think I'd stand a fighting chance with the skeleton. And that is all you can ever hope for in this life - a fighting chance.

*Friday, January 5, 2018*

Today is the one year anniversary of The Friendship Bridge Massacre. Mr. Chupka would let me use the term anniversary here. As an aside, I saw the Chupkanator on Washington Street the other day walking with an armful of firewood. Like everyone, he looked crazy thin, but it is real noticeable when you haven't seen somebody in a while. Mr. Chupka told me that he expected to see me back in school when all this was over. I promised him I would be there, and told him the great books I've been reading on my own. He seemed impressed.

As we talked on the street corner, I admitted to him that I was worried about what would come next, once the zombie pandemic was over. Mr. Chupka looked at me and said, "Everything will be OK. Remember, Jack. In the 14th century, after the Black Death came the Renaissance." I've kept repeating that in my head, "First the Plague, then the Renaissance." Before walking away, Mr. Chupka gave me some of his firewood, which is worth like way more than gold at this point. Still a cool guy - the Chupkanator.

Back to what I was saying about the anniversary of The Friendship Bridge Massacre - for an entire year dead humans have been reanimating as zombies, and attacking and killing healthy living humans. They don't need any weapons. They require no food, water, rest, or supplies of any kind. The zom just kill 24/7 and we can do nothing but protect our town from them. The world has been reduced to a quarter million trapped souls crammed into one square mile called Hoboken, New Jersey. Other pockets of survivors might exist, entire towns and cities fortified against the constant, endless attack like us. But we do not know of them, and our one attempt to reach others in the outside world miserably failed.

There is a small sense of hope, however, as the zom seem to be rotting into oblivion. They appear finally to be winding down, and we watch their approaching extinction with a sense of excitement and uncertainty. Once they are no longer a threat, what do we do? Just walk out of Hoboken and reclaim the world? It could take weeks, maybe even months for the threat to completely vanish. In the meantime, we have little food or firewood. And more importantly, we have no antibiotics for the thousands of people now sick with typhus. Can we wait out the zom? Hang on and survive a little while longer? I don't know. But it can't turn out that we came this far only to all die of typhus. Life couldn't be that cruel. Wait, did I just write that? After everything I've seen and experienced and lost, I'm surprised sometimes at my own stupidity.

Sunday, January 7, 2018

The snow is falling again. So, maybe it won't be the zom that ultimately do us in. Maybe it will be this new Ice Age. Or the typhus. Or starvation. Today I am experiencing nothing even close to hope. Typhus is now everywhere in Hoboken and people are afraid to venture out of their homes. The only good thing I can report is that the typical zom of 2018 is no match for its 2017 counterpart. They are fading as fast as we are, and from the lookout tower I just sit and watch them fall, skeletons crumbling in the snow.

I don't feel good today. I pretended for as long as I could that I was fine, but then I couldn't pretend any more once my fever spiked to 103. Mom is making me go to bed. When I think that this could be typhus, a sense of panic sweeps over me. I don't want to die. I acted like I didn't care before because I didn't really believe it was a possibility. Now it is a possibility and I want to be healthy again. I want to live. Luckily, I don't have a rash. And I'm sneezing and coughing, which aren't symptoms of typhus. I have to try and get some sleep. I'll write more when I feel better.

Sunday, January 14, 2018

That was one nasty head cold but I do feel better. I had some wild fever dreams that I can barely remember. Apparently, it was never typhus but maybe the flu. How could influenza have entered Hoboken after a year of little contact with the outside world? Maybe the zom brought it to the barricades and I caught it from them. Mom took good care of me all week. She has found her way back to totally, completely being our mother. We have aspirin so that helped keep my fever down.

Mostly, I just slept and dreamed - dreamed of Dad and Uncle Matt and Tolstoy, Mr. Rosen and Treblinka, life before the zom, life during the zom, the girl I "killed", zombie rat kings, Miranda and her mom, all of it racing in and out of my head. When I was awake, Miranda would read to me, which was wonderful. First we read *Frankenstein* by Mary Shelley (my choice). Then we read *Little Women* by Louisa May Alcott (her choice). Miranda said it was good for me to learn more about how girls think. I replied that I had already learned how girls think from reading Anne Frank. Between me and you, though, I really enjoyed *Little Women*. Crazy, man. Jo March was an incredibly cool girl, just like Anne. And like Katniss. And just like Miranda.

## Tuesday, January 16, 2018

I was thinking today about the six men and three women who made up the first group of scientists and astronauts stationed on the Moonbase Lunar Colony. Are they alive and well? Have they been watching the past twelve months play out around the globe? Will they ever be able to return to Earth since there will most likely not be a shuttle rocket sent to retrieve them? I guess they are ultimately our insurance that human beings will continue to exist.

There were also fourteen cosmonauts and astronauts from Russia, China, Israel, France, South Africa, Iran, India, and the United States up in the International Space Station when everything went down last January. These 23 people may turn out to be the only hope for a continuation of the species. Wow - 23! I never realized that before. Just like our doomed expedition. Crazy, man, for sure. I am very tired and going to sleep now.

## Thursday, January 18, 2018

I think whatever was happening between me and Miranda is not happening any more. Since her mother died and she moved in with us the relationship has morphed into more of a brother-sister thing than anything romantic. That's OK. It was a nice thing for a while, but nice things seem insignificant now. I feel the weight of the end of time all around me. I haven't been doing any scout shifts since I've been sick. Mom doesn't want me out there on the barricade in this cold, snowy weather. Miranda has also taken a break from the scouts. But there are plenty of other volunteers. Serena, Jason, Kahil, and Peter stop by from time to time and fill me in on the continued demise of the zom. I miss it. I miss them (my friends, my comrades, not the zom). I never had a greater sense of purpose in my life than when I guarded the gates of Hoboken from the zombie onslaught.

Even though I don't have typhus and I don't think the zom will finish us off after all, I have this sense that my days are numbered. I don't know how it will happen - my death - but I would be very surprised if one day I turned out to be an old man like Mr. Rosen. Strange that today is one of those days where the thought of dying doesn't freak me out so much. There are times when I imagine no longer existing on this planet and the fear and sadness of it overwhelms me. I'm glad today is not one of those days, because feeling strong and calm beats fear and sadness. I would pick strong and calm every time if I had the choice.

## Friday, January 19, 2018

You think you've seen the darkest days possible. Then today happens, and you realize there is no way to understand just how bad the next day can be. I was walking with Mom and Lily along Hudson Street this afternoon. We were heading back to our building. It was bitter cold with a sleety, icy rain coming down. Everyone we passed on the sidewalk was wrapped in scarves and bundled under tons of layers. Out of nowhere it happened, right in front of us at Hudson and 4th. Three people jumped together from the top floor of Marineview Plaza One, which is one of two 25-story apartment buildings that make up Marineview Plaza. They hit the ground less than a block from where we were walking. Mom and Lily screamed out of reflex, but I didn't make a sound. Though my heart felt like it stopped beating for a few seconds.

The three jumpers landed on a fourth person, an elderly woman hunched over pushing one of those folding metal grocery carts. I was watching this woman from a distance while we walked because she looked so sad and beaten down to me as she pushed her cart. That poor old woman. She made it so far in life, even survived a full year of the zom. Then three people who gave up and couldn't take it anymore chose the wrong moment to jump. It happened both quickly and slowly at the same time, if that makes any sense. Like it happened in slow motion but was over before I could really comprehend what I had seen. I'm trying not to think about the fact that if they had jumped a minute later they would have landed on us.

I know that tonight I will dream about the three jumpers and the old woman. How Mom and Lily screamed and I stood there in shock, despite everything I have witnessed the past year. I have seen zom in every stage of decomposition, but I'm used to that. Seeing four people and a metal grocery cart reduced to one mangled, bloody mess on the sidewalk was a new one for me. People have taken their own lives in Hoboken throughout the pandemic. I saw the river guard kill himself when he was bit by the female zom.

And before I started keeping this diary, I saw a man leap off Pier A into the Hudson River and drown himself. I've heard about the jumpers, including several from the W Hotel next door since it is so tall. But this was the first time I actually saw people jump with my own eyes. I never want to see that sight again.

## Saturday, January 20, 2018

New York City has become so quiet the past few days. Look at it across the Hudson. No more fires, not nearly as much loud guttural moaning, no movement whatsoever that we can see from here, even with the aid of Uncle Matt's telescope. There is still the stench. That will never disappear. And there is a low, faraway groaning that I assume is the sound of the zom slowly "dying". It sounds like wailing, the kind of sound a creature makes when it is fighting to not let go of life, which is crazy ironic. I suppose those zom reduced by now to nothing more than skeletons can barely manage even that low groaning and wailing, their jaw bones just clacking as they chomp at the air, appearing to catch the last of the winter flies that still surround them.

The zom may not be even remotely human, nothing more than walking reanimated corpses. But they do exist in some capacity. That must mean something to them. I feel at this moment, more so than ever since the zombie pandemic began, that I am sitting and waiting for the End of the World. If I am right then soon I will see my dad again. In Heaven. I have missed you so much, Dad. Never have two boys been more lucky than Ben and me because we had you as our father, even if we lost you sooner than was supposed to happen. I know it's just us, and our loss doesn't mean too much in a world with billions of losses. Still, today I'm feeling like a boy whose father died in a world where everyone else has two parents. Crazy, man, to feel that way now.

## Sunday, January 21, 2018

We're all so weak. Food is running out and winter shows no signs of letting up and giving us an early spring. I am cold and hungry and worn out, tired of trying to outlive the zom. I am ready to die, to curl up in a ball in the corner of the room and say "that's it." Just wait for the sleep to overtake me. And have a night of dreaming that ends not with morning in Hoboken during a zombie apocalypse, but with the endless white clouds of heaven, reunited with Dad and Uncle Matt and Jed and Tolstoy and Brendan and Grandma and Ryan and Mr. Rosen and Suzanne and Mrs. Jelinek and Officer Sanchez and our 23 doomed explorers and the man I watched jump off the pier to drown and the river guard who shot himself after he was bit and the three people who leapt from Marineview Plaza One and the old woman they landed on and the girl I "killed" to save Jason.

In Heaven I would also get to meet Anne Frank. I would thank her for the strength she gave me with her words this past year, and tell her how sorry I am that she and her sister and parents and friends were murdered the way they were. She deserved life, as I deserve life. Like all fourteen and fifteen year kids, we had a right to the future they told us about in childhood. Why did our parents promise us that everything would work out? That the future was ours to conquer? I believe it's OK to give up when enough is enough, when you are trapped in a winter that will never end. I'm going to bed now, and I am not afraid to not wake up.

## Monday, January 22, 2018

I did wake up this morning, after all. I am still alive here in Hoboken, New Jersey. Morning dawned despite my wishes and despite the zom. First thing, I went up on the roof. Though a cold day, the sun was shining and the rays felt wonderful hitting my face. Interestingly, there were no sounds at all coming from Manhattan, not even the low, faraway cry of the zom disappearing into history and oblivion. This is the first day I can remember without any guttural moaning. Not even the faintest hint of it carried with the wind.

After lunch, which consisted of raw turnips and edible winter weeds gathered in the park, Mom and I walked together to the barricade on Observer Highway to take a look at the other side. I wanted to see how things had changed during the month. The sun was brilliantly bright as we made our way from River Street. We both climbed up into the lookout tower. Serena, Jason and Kahil squeezed close together to make room for us. Mom had never looked before at no man's land. Skeletons and dismembered, disfigured, rotting corpses crawled by us below. They don't even try to penetrate the barricade any more. As Mom stared in disbelief at the abandoned cars, endless debris, and parade of crawling zom, we heard a rumbling in the distance, like how an earthquake must feel. Serena spotted them first with her binoculars.

"Tanks!" she screamed. "I see army tanks coming this way!!"

Jason sounded the air horn and we watched in silence, uncertain who or what might be inside the tanks as they rolled towards Hoboken. I stopped counting at thirty tanks and there were more on the horizon. I think it was a full armored division. They rolled right over what was left of the zom, crushing their skulls, and stopped short of plowing through the barricade itself. A soldier appeared out of one of the turrets. He announced himself as a general and shouted up to us that we were liberated. Mom and Serena and Jason and Kahil and I were all speechless. I thought for a second that I was in the middle of another fever dream. But it was real. Liberation had arrived.

As it turns out, Tony's shortwave radio broadcasts actually reached someone and brought us help. The United States Army Installation at Fort Meade in Maryland survived the zombie apocalypse and received Tony's broadcasts. They knew we were here and they were finally able to make their way to us as the zom "died off". The USS New York and the USS Arlington, both out at sea when everything went down last year, are on their way to us as I write these words.

Hoboken has erupted into celebration. A quarter million people on their collective last leg, dying from starvation and typhus and the end of all hope, are now dancing in the streets. It reminds me of Mr. Rosen's stories from the end of World War II, stepping from the depths of darkness into the faint light of tomorrow. Mom and Ben and Lily and Lok and Miranda and Ginger and I made it to this day that I thought would never come, this first day on the other side of the Year of the Zom. I always said this was the diary of a zombie scout, written to preserve the story of life in Hoboken during this awful, sad, ugly time. Now that liberation has arrived, the need for this diary is thankfully gone. I may start a new journal, possibly a novel, but I am done writing in these pages. Time to think about the future and let go of the zombie past. Time to get on with life. The end. And the beginning. . . .

# EPILOGUE

It has been forty years since the Year of the Zom. The corpses have long been cleared out of our towns and cities, hundreds of millions of them, actually billions, reduced in the end to skeletons and bits of rotted flesh. The blood-borne virus that caused all of this death and destruction disappeared into the annals of human history with the last reanimated corpse. No one knows what triggered it on January 5, 2017, on the Friendship Bridge between Uzbekistan and Afghanistan. My guess is no one will ever know. But the world is once again back in motion, spinning toward a future filled with possibility and hope. Two generations have been born since 2017 and they only know this world. Not the world that existed before the zom, and not the world that existed in 2017 and early 2018 when survival was a day to day struggle.

My family stayed in Hoboken for the rest of my childhood. Mom moved us into a larger apartment once the population decreased as people began to venture out of town.

Miranda remained with us as our adopted sister. Jack's brief romance with her became a thing of the past that they often laughed about in the years that followed. Miranda's father never returned home for her. London did not survive the zombie apocalypse after all, like most places on the planet. Dad and Uncle Matt never came home either. I think Mom and Jack and I each made peace with that even before the soldiers arrived to liberate us. I should add that Jack's friend Ryan, who he wrote about in these pages, was also never heard from again. As was the case with my mother's family in Texas. All gone. Swallowed up by the zombie maelstrom. More people died than lived. That is the reality of what happened in 2017.

Lily and Lok both remained in Hoboken during those initial years as we humans rebuilt society around the globe. Lily married a great guy, one of our liberating soldiers, Major Roger P. Dunworthy of Athens, Georgia, and together they had three daughters - Caroline (named after Lily's Mom), Jenny and Becca (both named after Lily's sisters). Lily and her husband also adopted two boys orphaned by the zom, Tim and Jamie. Lok completed an engineering degree at Stevens Tech and did quite well for himself during the years of rebuilding. He worked on the shuttle project that returned our 23 astronauts to us from the Moonbase Lunar Colony and the International Space Station. Like Lily, Lok also married a great guy, Greg, who survived 2017 on an isolated farm in Upstate New York with nine other people.

Lok and Greg adopted and raised six orphaned children in the Washington, D.C. area - Meghan, David, Vanessa, Carlos, Andrew, and Aliyah. I still see both Lily and Lok often.

Miranda married as well, strangely to of all people Peter Conner, who arrived with his family from West Orange and became a zombie scout. They found their way to each other several years after 2017, and had four children, two boys and two girls. The boys were named Michael and Justin (after Miranda's father and Peter's oldest brother, who was away at college when everything went down and never came home). The girls were named Amy and Kate (after Miranda's mother and my mother).

Serena, Jason and Kahil all stayed in Hoboken with their families during their teenage years and remained good friends with Jack. Serena became a pediatrician and moved to Boston with her husband, whom she met in medical school. They had six children, four boys and two girls. After college, Jason moved to San Diego and Kahil to Chicago. Like Jack, they both enlisted in the Civilian Redevelopment Corps. As with so many of their generation who survived the zombie pandemic, they wanted to play a part in forging a new nation. Finally, our dear friend and faithful pet Ginger lived another twelve years after 2017 before dying in her sleep one night in the autumn of 2029. We did not know Ginger's actual age when she came to us, but in the end she seemed pretty old. She was a good girl till her last days and I miss her still.

As everyone is aware, New York was not cleared for civilians to re-enter until 2025. Other big cities like Los Angeles, Houston, Miami, Atlanta, Phoenix, New Orleans, St. Louis, Cleveland, Mexico City, Caracas, Rio de Janeiro, Paris, Rome, Berlin, Budapest, Prague, Moscow, Cairo, Istanbul, Tehran, Mumbai, Beijing, Bangkok, and many, many others were closed to the outside world for almost as long.

I remember when we were able to finally travel into Manhattan again for the first time. I was 16 and Jack was 22. We took a hovercraft across the Hudson River on a clear, cold winter day and made our way to Cornelia Street to Uncle Matt's apartment. Once inside, we found behind the couch the skeleton of a small animal. We assumed it was Tolstoy. He must have suffered so, the poor little guy, alone by himself in the end with no one to love him or feed him. Uncle Matt must have gone out by himself for some reason when he was bit. I always imagined Uncle Matt carrying Tolstoy in his cat case, running with Dad to the ferry when the zom got them. At least we learned a small part of what truly happened when we found Tolstoy's remains.

Jack and I scooped up Tolstoy's bones and took them back to Hoboken in a small sack. We kept them wrapped in a velvet cloth in that same sack, hidden away at the back of Mom's closet. When Ginger died a few years later, we buried Tolstoy with her up in the Catskills. Property law and inheritance rights back then were not what they were before 2017, or what they are again today. Squatting and homesteading were common since most property did not have anyone returning to stake a claim. Mr. Rosen had left us the key to his cabin in Phoenicia in Upstate New York, and so we claimed it as ours. I believe he would have wanted that. Ginger and Tolstoy are buried there. As is my mother. And Jack.

The years after 2017 were no easier for us than they were for anyone else. We found out later that there were many pockets of survivors, numerous fortified Hobokens dotting the landscape of America. Around the world some bigger cities managed to survive largely intact, such as Auckland, New Zealand; Perth, Western Australia; Santiago, Chile; Vancouver, Canada; Sarajevo, Bosnia and Herzegovina; Cape Town, South Africa; Reykjavik, Iceland; Seattle, Washington; and Honolulu, Hawaii. And there were the miracles of Ireland and Madagascar - two islands not touched at all by the zombie pandemic except for the multitude of refugees each welcomed to its shores. We did the best we could during those lawless decades that followed to make our way in an often unpredictable and violent world. It was difficult at times to say when we were more in danger. During the time of the zom or in the years that followed when a Wild West mentality prevailed?

On Saturday, April 7, 2035, Jack and his old friend Tony Degrassi were about to enter a bar on the Lower East Side of Manhattan when they were approached by a gang of armed thugs. It should have been a simple robbery with

Tony and Jack surviving after their money and valuables were taken. But as Tony described it to us later, Jack fought back, refusing to give up our father's watch to the robbers. He paid with his life, suffering a knife wound to the chest that caused him to bleed to death in Tony's arms on Hester Street. His last words were, "Look out for Mom and Ben for me." He thought about us until his last breath.

Once he was gone, I took several years to regain my footing. His death devastated all of us. I truly believe it was Jack's death and not the cancer that killed Mom. Even now, I can recall as if it was yesterday Jack crawling into bed with me on those hot summer nights in 2017 when I was so afraid of the guttural moaning that echoed from across the river. He would lull me to sleep with stories about the Moonbase Lunar Colony, and how we would make our way there together and live a long and happy life far away from the zom. How I miss him! But I survived the loss of Jack as I survived every other loss of my life. There is no choice to do otherwise. If Jack taught me anything - and he taught me much - it is never to give up, despite his claim at times in this diary that he was giving up. The difference for me with this loss was that I was no longer alone. I had my wonderful wife, Laura, to help me through it, and our boys, Teddy and Matt. I think just about every child born after 2017 has been named for someone who never returned home that fateful year.

After his death, I retrieved this diary from Jack's brownstone on Perry Street in the West Village of Manhattan. Jack was one of those brave pioneers trying to rebuild America's greatest city. It would not exist as the vibrant, bustling metropolis it is today without the likes of Jack Sullivan. Now that there is again a publishing industry and the internet, and people are writing and buying books, I thought the time had come for *Zombie Scout: The Diary of Jack Sullivan*. It may not be considered distinguished Nobel or Pulitzer Prize winning literature, but it is an honest account of one boy trying to find his way to manhood during the most challenging chapter in human history. I have not changed a single word, not a single comma or period. This is Jack's diary, exactly as he wrote. Exactly as he intended for you to read it. The only thing I added was the dedication "for my brother" as well as the bold and italicized lines at the beginning setting place and time in the context of the zombie pandemic.

Let us never forget 2017 and everyone we lost during those dark, dark days. As we forge ahead with a new society, let us continue to remember the old society that perished, all that was good as well as all that was less than good about it. We must honor both those things. Let us also extend our eternal gratitude to the City of Seattle. The people of that great metropolis, the largest city on the mainland of the United States to survive the Year of the Zom, rose to the occasion and acted as this nation's capitol for almost two decades when it was needed most. Now our national government sits again on the banks of the Potomac in Washington D.C. with the President occupying the White House and Congress at work on Capitol Hill.

We are once more a great nation. Actually, we were never anything less, especially in 2017 and 2018. Perhaps, as during the Civil War and the Great Depression and World War II and the attacks of 9/11, we are at our very best when things are worst, to borrow and paraphrase a line from one of Jack's favorite old movies, *Starman* with Jeff Bridges. May you each continue to find happiness and hope as we get on with the important work of rebuilding our world. God bless America. God bless Planet Earth. And God bless each and every one of you, both the survivors of the Great Zombie Plague as well as all the children who have come after

*– Congressman Ben Sullivan (D-NJ)*
*Washington D.C., 2057*